Rule 17

And who had kno[...]
the boss, as he'd e[...]
night, as he'd kissed her and held her and—

'We both know the rule, *Mr* Cunningham,' Carrie
said, her voice a mixture of hurt and anger. 'So
what was last night all about?'

He saw the sheen of tears in Carrie's hurt green
eyes, but he couldn't tell her what he wanted to
say. That last night was about feelings he'd never
felt before, about a oneness he never thought
possible. He should have said goodnight at her
door, but he'd said goodnight as they were drifting
off to sleep, naked and sated...

Dear Reader,

Merry Christmas from all of us at Silhouette Desire®! To celebrate, we've got an extra special line-up for you to enjoy over the holiday season.

We begin with Jackie Merritt's MAN OF THE MONTH, *Montana Christmas*, which is the conclusion of her spectacular MADE IN MONTANA series. Then Scarlett Morgan gets a lot more than she bargained for from her new business partner Colin Slater in *A Bride for Crimson Falls*, which is the third title in Cindy Gerard's mini-series NORTHERN LIGHTS BRIDES.

Gabriel's Bride by Suzannah Davis is a classic—and sensuous—love story you're sure to enjoy, and Anne Eames demonstrates a delightful writing style in *Christmas Elopement. Love-Child* by Metsy Hingle is a wonderful tale about reunited lovers, and Kate Little's *Jingle Bell Baby* will make you feel all the warmth and goodwill of the holiday season.

Have a fantastic time!

The Editors

Christmas Elopement

ANNE EAMES

™ SILHOUETTE

Desire ®

Silhouette, Silhouette Desire and Colophon
are registered trademarks of Harlequin Books S.A.,
used under licence.

First published in Great Britain 1997
Silhouette Books, Eton House, 18-24 Paradise Road,
Richmond, Surrey TW9 1SR

© Creative Business Services, Inc. 1996

ISBN 0 373 76042 6

22-9712

Printed and bound in Great Britain
by Mackays of Chatham PLC, Chatham

ANNE EAMES

says her energetic imagination has been fuelled by her motley background, which includes theatre sales and construction management—collectively providing her with a plethora of ideas for a lifetime of stories.

Anne and her engineer husband, Bill, live in southeastern Michigan and share a family of five—two hers (Tim and Tom), two his (Erin and David), and one theirs (an adorable miniature dachshund, Punkin).

Other novels by Anne Eames

Silhouette Desire®

Two Weddings and a Bride
You're What?!

To Julia Cameron for her book *The Artist's Way*,
which has changed forever the way I approach my craft,
and
To those enlightened employers,
managers and supervisors everywhere
who contribute to the happiness and well-being
of their employees

One

So here it was, Friday the thirteenth. Bad hair, no fiancé, no job, and she felt like she was going to puke for the third time this morning. Tuesday's flu was no longer the cause. More likely it was the bottle of cheap wine she'd consumed last night during a rare self-indulgent blue funk.

She should have known it would be a lousy week. So far, the bad perm on Monday had been the best part. She grabbed chunks of hair in each hand and growled in frustration. It was dry, fuzzy, bushy. Totally out of control. Unmanageable. Just like her ramshackle life.

"Oh, heiferdust! You really don't have time for this self-pity, Carrie Sargent." Where were those old problem-solving skills of hers, anyway?

She munched on a soda cracker, licking the salt from her lips. The teapot whistled, and she poured the steaming water over a tea bag and gave it a few dunks. Mug in hand, she stared out at the foggy mist that hung over Monterey Bay and the Cannery, far below. It was a view to be envied and one that she'd miss, but she had to move. No two ways about it. It might be some time before her lodgings rivaled her recent life-style, but Carmel wasn't too shabby. If she had to climb off this mountain, there were worse places she could go.

Earlier in the week she'd actually considered the option of letting Brian bail her out—a small loan till she found a new job. Brian. She scoffed at the mere thought of her ex-fiancé. Last night, before she could even broach the subject, he'd whipped out his checkbook in that superior way of his and summarily categorized her problem as "typically female." So before the night was over, she'd summarily slapped his grandmother's priceless three-carat marquise diamond in his hand and told him to take a hike.

That was a mistake, she thought now, eyeing another cracker. She should have kept the ring.

The phone beside her jangled and she jumped, the movement sending shock waves through her pounding head, her stomach rolling over again. If it was Brian or her landlord, she didn't have the time or energy. She was tempted to let it ring, but then she worried that it might be about today's job interview.

Another curse and she lifted the receiver. "Hello?"

"Carrie, it's Brian."

Why did he always identify himself? Like she wouldn't know? "Brian who?" she snapped.

"Oh, for God sake's, Carrie, you need me—"

"Need you?" she said, letting the acid in her mouth spike her tone.

"Yes," he said, his usual arrogance seeping through the receiver. "For many things...not the least of which is money."

That was Brian. Forever the romantic. What had she ever seen in this jerk—besides his good looks, intelligence and wealth? Was she that shallow?

"What if you don't get that job today?" he continued, sounding confident he was gaining ground. "May I remind you, Ms. S, your landlord has served you with Notice To Quit? If you don't come up with the rent by next week—"

"Enough, Brian. I don't need your money *or* your reminders." She heard the anger in her raised voice, and quickly reined it in. In a much more controlled tone, she finished swiftly. "Save the arguments for your next jury, Counselor." Before he could reply, she hung up the phone and turned on the answering machine.

The start-up beep had barely sounded when the phone rang again. Quickly she turned down the volume. There was no point getting riled up about things. They'd said it all before. Again and again. If last night had been their first major setback, maybe... But it hadn't. She snatched up another cracker and snapped open the morning paper.

The front page detailed the latest disaster. She flipped to the comics, searching for a quick laugh, finding a chuckle in "Marmaduke." Finally, after another cup of tea and a fruitless tour of the classifieds, she reread the ad clipped for today's interview. It was long and detailed. Nothing in it ruled her out. And everything about it sounded good. In fact, too good to be true.

The answering machine picked up another call and Carrie frowned at her ringless third finger. With a weary sigh, she shoved out of the chair and headed for the shower. If she could just keep the crackers and tea down long enough to get dressed and out the door...

When she walked outside an hour later, sunlight had burned off the fog, and her smile widened. A mischievous sensation arched her brow as she fussed with the lucky scarf at her neck. It was a watercolor flurry of kelly green and carrot orange—perfect matches to her eyes and hair. Probably navy or basic black would have been a safer choice.

"Oh, well."

She tucked the colorful scarf under the lapel of her salmon-colored suit and settled behind the wheel of her rusted Woodie station wagon. This outfit was far more fun, she'd convinced herself, one that was certain to stand out among the other corporate types. She turned the key and the car coughed and sputtered before turning over.

"Besides, S, when have you ever played it safe? When did caution ever enter into the equation?" She smiled through the bug-spattered windshield and snaked her way down toward the city.

Yep. With her experience and references, she'd get that job. If not today, by the next interview. She'd better. She was down to her last hundred bucks. After the interview she'd go talk to Gus at Day's Pub in Carmel. One way or the other she'd find a way to work things out. She cranked down the window, turned up the Mozart and clutched the wheel of her Woodie for dear life, willing away the butterflies in her stomach.

Tourist traffic had picked up now that the holidays were drawing near, making the trek a slow one, giving her time to enjoy the late-fall air and the ever-present trade winds that wafted through the window. Cunningham Construction was a couple of blocks away. She glanced at her watch: ten minutes till eleven. Plenty of time.

Twenty minutes later she darted around the last construction barricade, yanked the steering wheel a hard right into the parking lot and ran smack-dab into the front fender of a Mercedes convertible. She jerked against the seat belt, and her head whipped back, soda crackers revisiting the back of her throat. The sickening sound of dimpling metal reverberated in her already aching head.

Great! Just what she needed. She did a quick inventory of her body parts and found none bleeding, so she flung open the door to inspect Woodie. The left fender looked like she felt. Mean and ugly. The other car looked a little like Brian's, only this one was black instead of navy. Probably another lawyer, she thought, as she spun on the guilty driver.

"Look what you've done!" she shouted at the black suit and wing tips, not having made her way to his face yet.

"What *I've* done! You're the one driving like a bat out of hell!"

"I had the right-of-way. I was turning right."

"Except I was already there."

Carrie glanced at the tanned face, her words lost momentarily. Drop-dead gorgeous. The sun bounced off his black hair like a halo. Blue eyes were invading her space. She stepped back and regrouped.

"I'm in a hurry. Just write out your insurance information and I'll do the same." There. She was in control again. Although he hesitated a moment, his jaw muscles working overtime, he did what she asked.

They exchanged papers and then, with slitted glances flitting between them in an angry duel, they returned to their vehicles. He pulled away first, backing off Woodie, loosening the front bumper in the process.

"Damn!" Would this week ever be over? Slowly she pulled into the lot, the bumper scraping the blacktop in a cry for help. She got out and walked to the front of it, taking a long, slow look.

"Oh, Woodie, look what he's done to you. No respect for the elderly, that one. Well, just wait till he hears from my insurance company!"

She straightened her scarf and her shoulders and quickened her pace to the front door. She hated being late. She was never late. First the construction, now this.

A large three-story atrium greeted her when she walked through the door, the only decoration a huge brass sculpture suspended overhead. Off-white concrete walls, no photos, no plants. She headed for the elevator, her heels echoing on the pristine hardwood floor. The secretary had said the third floor, so she punched the number and made her ascent.

The name Cunningham Construction was displayed in dense brass letters behind a reception area that was also de-

void of color or warmth. Not even a hint of the impending
holidays. The young woman behind the desk, however,
smiled warmly when Carrie approached her.

"Carrie Sargent?" she asked, still smiling.

"Yes. I'm sorry I'm late, but—"

The woman waved her hand. "Not to worry. The boss
just got here himself. He said the construction down there
has everything tied up. Would you like some coffee?"

She'd like some more tea, but with her luck she'd spill it
all over herself or the interviewer. "No, thank you."

"I just handed him your résumé. Let me see if he's
ready."

Carrie watched her disappear around the corner and exhaled a slow breath. Time for an attitude adjustment. The
week so far might have been lousy, but she needed this job.
This could be the turning point she was hoping for....

"You may go in now, Ms. Sargent," the young woman
said when she returned, then added softly under her breath.
"He's not in the best mood this morning, but his bark is
worse than his bite. He's really a nice guy when you get to
know him."

"Thanks for the warning," Carrie whispered back, her
lower intestines contracting. Great. Just great.

"First door on the right," the secretary called over her
shoulder.

The man sitting behind the desk had his back to her,
staring out the glass wall behind him. She put on her best
smile and rapped softly on the open oak door beside her.

He swiveled around abruptly, as if roused from some
trance.

"You!" he said, blue eyes widening.

Carrie's chances for a quick paycheck dimmed along with
her smile. Nonetheless, she stepped forward and extended
her hand. "Carrie Sargent. I'm here about the job."

He looked at her hand a moment, then stood and gave it
one quick shake before dropping back into his tan leather
chair. His lips were locked tight and his dark eyebrows

pinched together. His gaze drifted to her bright scarf and suit, then back to her eyes.

"Is this how you always dress for an interview, or do you save this getup for demolition-derby days?"

She folded her arms and shifted her weight to one foot. The job was obviously out the window, so why hold back? "Is this how you talk to your employees, or do you save your arrogance for lowly applicants?"

He slapped his palms on the desk and pushed out of his chair. "I think you can assume this interview is over, Miss...Miss..."

"Sargent." She retrieved the insurance information from her pocket and read the name he'd scribbled early. Cash Cunningham—President. Made sense. It was that kind of week. "Well, Mr. Cunningham, I'd like to say it's been a pleasure to meet you, but I've never been a good liar." She turned to go, throwing a last line over her shoulder. "Expect to hear from my insurance company."

Cash watched the curly carrot-colored hair bounce off the woman's shoulders as she stormed off, then crumpled her résumé and tossed it in the corner wastebasket. For this he'd rushed back from a job site?

Suddenly she was in the doorway again, hands on hips. "Do you suppose you could find some twine or something to tie up the bumper you destroyed?"

Of all the gall. He had a mind to sit her in the chair and tie *her* up, this loose cannon with the face full of freckles and legs up to—

He picked up the phone and punched the intercom to the warehouse. "Sam...got a lady here who needs help." That was an understatement. "Find some twine and meet her in the parking lot. She'll be easy to spot. Just look for a gaudy suit next to an old rust-bucket wagon." He hung up the receiver and took some pleasure from the steam generating off the body in the doorway. She was glaring at him, her ample chest rising and falling rapidly as she mouthed words that challenged his heritage. Swinging her hair off her shoulders, she disappeared again.

Cash steepled his fingers and waited, half expecting another visit. When none came, he buzzed his secretary, who stood in front of him a moment later.

"Obviously, *that* one didn't work out," he said. "Are more scheduled?"

"Not really. Miss Sargent sounded so nice on the phone, and her references raved about her. Sorry, boss. I thought I found you a winner."

She was a winner, all right. Cash heaved a sigh. "Go through the pile again and see if we overlooked anyone." Peggy started to leave. "Oh, and Peg . . . if you don't find anything, then give that headhunter a call . . . Dwayne what's-his-name?"

"Dwayne Flutie," she said.

"Right. Flutie." Damn! He hated giving those bloodsuckers money. "On second thought, Peg, wait till Monday's mail. If we don't have a candidate by then, find Flutie and I'll talk to him."

"Aye, aye, boss," Peggy said, rolling her eyes as she turned.

Cash grabbed a handful of paper from his in-basket and swore under his breath. All this paperwork was killing him. If he didn't get someone soon, he'd drown in it.

Peg was already in over her head, but just two years out of high school, what did he expect? She was good on the phone, dealing with customers and directing the hundreds of calls they received. There was little time for anything else. Besides, when he hired her, he'd known she was light on experience and it would be years before she was ready for much more. Still, the price was right. She seemed happy with a little over minimum wage and benefits after a year.

He rifled through the pile in front of him, knowing he'd have to cancel tomorrow's golf game. If he was lucky, maybe he'd find his desk under all this mess by Sunday night. And sometime over the weekend he had to see about car repairs, thanks to that... that...spitfire. He leaned back, locked his hands behind his head and emitted a sardonic laugh.

When was the last time someone had dressed him down like that? Ever? He couldn't remember anything quite like it.

Two
────

Carrie made a pit stop at the insurance adjuster's office, where she got the bad news about hard-to-find parts, plus a reminder that she'd changed her deductible to two hundred and fifty dollars—which was more than double the amount left in her pocket.

Cursing her luck, she headed for Carmel and M. M. Day's Pub. By the time she found a parking space a half hour later she was in a real snit. With long strides she marched to the bar, hopped up on a stool, crossed her arms on the scarred mahogany counter and waited for Gus to notice her, which took only a few seconds.

"Carrie, my love. What can I getcha?" He reached out and patted her arm, a warm smile crinkling the corners of his tired eyes.

"Coffee, please." It had been months since she'd stopped by to see him. Now she felt guilty about the favor she was about to ask. "How's it going, Gus?"

"Oh, I can't complain. How's your pop doin'? Does he like Maine?"

"He's getting better every day. Says he loves being back east after all these years."

"Thank the Lord, no paralysis, huh?" He deposited a steaming mug in front of her.

"You can say that again! There's still a little speech problem, but nothing you can't understand—especially when he starts swearing." She chuckled, feeling the frustrations of the morning slip away. "Yep, that always comes out crystal-clear. Sometimes I hear him giving the visiting nurse the what-for, so I guess he's pretty much back to normal." She sipped her coffee and sighed. "Mmm...Thanks, Gus. I needed this."

"Bad day?" He dried glasses as he spoke.

"Bad week." She tucked a handful of frizz behind each ear and blew at her bangs.

"Sorry to hear that, Carrie. Real shame you lost your job when your pop's business sold. He always boasted what a fine job you did. Find anythin' new yet?" A customer waved at the far end of the bar and Gus motioned he'd be right back.

Carrie's gaze trailed after him, then wandered to the frame-filled walls. Everywhere she looked there were photographs of Clint Eastwood in movies that spanned decades, some autographed, many with props or costumes encased alongside. She'd seen him here a few times visiting with Gus, surrounded by heavy-breathing females. If only he were a little younger and would sweep in here now and make her day.

Fat chance.

Well, this was it. No more stalling. Time for a little humble pie. God, she hadn't waited tables since she was a teenager. She glanced around the room and found another thirty-something waitress and felt a little better. The lunch crowd had thinned. Now was as good a time as any.

Gus came around the end of the bar and took a stool next to her. She swiveled toward him, eyes cast down.

"If you're here for a little help—" Gus took both her hands in his and squeezed gently "—I told your pop I'd keep an eye on ya. What can I do, lass?"

Carrie forced her gaze level with his, blinking clear her vision. "I was hoping you might need another waitress...just for a while...till I get back on my feet."

Gus scratched the stubble on his cheek and studied her out of the corner of his eye.

"I'd work whatever hours you've got...bartend, too, if you want. I know it's been a long time since I did any of this, but I'll pick it up again—"

"Whoa." Gus held up both hands. "You don't let a guy get a word in edgewise." He chuckled and she knew she had the job. "I was just thinkin' about something else."

"Like?"

"Like..." He hesitated, looking embarrassed, but then continued. "Like if you need to work here, then maybe ya can't afford your house in Monterey, either." He lowered his head and arched his brows, acting as if he'd pried but daring her to deny it.

"Well, you're right." Now it was her turn to be embarrassed. "I have to find a new place. Soon."

"It's not much, but there's a room upstairs...got a sofa bed and little dinette set...and a bathroom with a shower stall, no tub."

"When can I move in?" She could barely contain her excitement. At last her luck was turning.

"As soon as I get someone to clean it up—"

"Oh, I can do that." Carrie jumped off the stool and threw her arms around Gus's neck. "You're a lifesaver, Gus McGee."

He patted her on the back and chuckled. As she pulled away and planted a kiss on his forehead, he asked, "When do you wanna start work?"

"Tonight, if you need me."

"Go home and pack your stuff, Carrie girl, and I'll have someone clean upstairs." She started to argue but Gus cut her off. "When ya get settled in, we'll talk about your work schedule, okay?"

She held up her index finger. "One condition."

Gus narrowed his gaze. "And what might that be, lassie?"

"That you apply my wages toward rent."

"I'll do nothing of the kind. How will you live?"

"If I'm any good at my job, hopefully I'll get tips." Gus was shaking his head vigorously, but she persisted. "Besides, this is only temporary. I'll be getting an office job soon enough. Then I'll pay you rent like a normal person."

Carrie stilled his head between her fingers and stopped his protest. "Gus . . . I'm a big girl now, and I've got my pride. Please?"

He took her hands in his once again. "You're just as pig-headed as your pop, lassie." He smoothed a stray lock of hair from her cheek and smiled. "And just as beautiful as your mama, God rest her soul." He stood at last, pulling her into a gentle embrace before returning to his post behind the bar.

"Well?" he said, after a moment. "What are ya doin' sittin' around here lookin' all misty-eyed? Don't ya have boxes to pack?"

Sunday afternoon Carrie darted in front of the big screen, trying not to obstruct the game behind her. M. M. Day's was filled to capacity with San Francisco 49ers fans cheering or booing each play of the game. The team was beating the Detroit Lions handily, which meant the crowd was in a good mood. Beer and tips flowed freely. She'd only been patted on the backside once so far.

Funny how the only accident she'd had was in that guy's lap.

Well, it'd been a long time since she'd carried such a heavy tray, Gus explained to the irate patron as he left for home in search of dry clothes. Gus returned to the bar and Carrie placed another order, busying herself with cherries, olives and the like, ignoring Gus's probing stare.

"So, lass...is that how you'll handle anyone who gets too friendly?"

She grabbed a handful of cocktail napkins and kept her eyes cast down. "Probably," she said, knowing full well she would.

Gus lifted her chin with his finger and looked at her sternly. "Do you suppose when the next *accident* happens you could have just one or two drinks on the tray and no food?"

A laugh burst from Carrie's lips. "I suppose that could be arranged."

He dropped his hand from her face and chuckled. "That geezer's been a thorn in my backside for years. Don't know why I never did that myself."

His gaze left hers and she turned to see what had caught his attention. A young, prissy-looking man in a Brooks Brothers suit had settled into the corner booth by the window, far from the game and the men in jeans.

"Do you know that man?" Carrie asked.

"Afraid so. Comes in fairly regular. Orders salads and Perrier, which is fine with me. But he likes to talk. Gossips about everything and everyone and expects me to sit down and visit." Gus looked back at Carrie and grinned. "Gee, the boys watchin' the game are motionin' for me, lass. Why don't you go introduce yourself to Dwayne over there. Take a break. Talk to him about opera or somethin'. That'll make him happy." Gus patted Carrie on the shoulder as he passed, seeming pleased that he'd dodged the bullet.

Carrie watched the little man in the corner with a critical eye. He seemed harmless enough. Kind of reminded her of Dr. Niles Crane on the sitcom "Frasier." She couldn't help but wonder what brought him here. He looked as out of place as Rush Limbaugh at a Democratic fund raiser. Curiosity piqued, she strolled over.

"Can I get you something?" she started, taking a closer look at his precisely cut blond hair and deep-set brown eyes.

He lifted his chin and managed to talk down at her, even from his lower position. "I think I'll do something daring and have a cup of clam chowder."

Carrie bit the inside of her cheek. "And to drink?"

"Oh, some of that wonderfully flavored iced tea of yours, I think. Yes, yes. Bring me a tall frosted glass of it, please." He closed his menu and handed it to her, cocking his head to one side. "You're new here, aren't you?"

"Yes. As of this weekend. It's temporary, though . . . till I find something in my field." His snobbishness had drawn the same from her. She scribbled his order and started to leave.

"Wait!"

She turned back and saw a rectangular smile of perfect teeth. With long, deliberate fingers he withdrew a gold case from his breast pocket, removed a business card and presented it to her with great flair.

She read it and said, "Ahhh . . . a headhunter."

His back straightened. "I prefer to think of myself as a management placement professional."

She was sure he did. She shot him a phony smile. "I'll get your order."

When she returned with the soup and tea she noticed a legal pad in front of Dwayne, a Waterman rollerball pen poised between his fingers. He nodded to the seat across from him. With only the slightest hesitation, she obliged. Why not? Maybe he could find her something similar to the opening at Cunningham Construction. She thought about telling dandy Dwayne what had happened last Friday, but decided against it.

Monday morning Peggy peered around the corner and Cash motioned her in. "I'm afraid to ask. . . . Anything?"

Peggy wrinkled her nose and tossed her short blond hair from side to side. "Sorry, boss...but I did as you suggested. Dwayne Flutie is on line two."

Cash looked at the ceiling and blew out a stream of hot air. The last time he used the guy it had cost the company over twenty grand in finder's fees. However, he had located a good project manager—one who was still around and was a hell of a worker. "Okay, Peg. Thanks."

Cash watched her scurry away before he picked up the phone.

Ten minutes later he hung up, stunned by the speed and efficiency with which Flutie had handled him. He had actually agreed to join the guy for dinner at some pub in Carmel. How was it he'd put it?

Oh, yes—"to meet just the woman you need."

At 7:25 Cash parked his loaner a block past M. M. Day's and slammed the door. He shook his head at its garish red color and made a mental note to call the garage in the morning. Hopefully the parts were readily available and he'd have his own wheels sometime soon. He strode the short distance to the entrance and found Flutie in a booth by the window. He half stood and held out his hand as Cash slid in across from him.

"Kind of you to join me on such short notice, Cash," he said over a limp shake, then sat down and got right to business. "I have a résumé here that I'm sure you'll find very impressive." He slid it in front of Cash and leaned back, chin high, shoulders too straight.

Cash forced his gaze away from this strange little character to the paper in front of him. He'd read so many résumés the past few weeks that they all looked the same. Skipping the top portion, he went right to the experience section. He was prepared for a nice, neat format, good grammar and no substance. What he saw was fifteen years at a construction company—a woman who had worked her way from the bottom to management in nice steady steps.

He even recognized the name of one of her references—a well-respected developer he'd done business with a few years back. As much as he hated to admit it, Flutie might have something here.

"Well, Dwayne," he said, "when do I get to meet her?"

Three

Carrie flew down the back inside stairway, then stopped at the connecting door. She inhaled and exhaled three deep breaths, then yanked the handle inward. Gus gave her a low whistle as she paused at the bar.

"You look terrific, lass. If your résumé hasn't already sold the guy, how can he resist the prettiest gal in Carmel?"

Carrie emitted a not too convinced chuckle. "I think your opinion is a tad biased, Gus McGee," she said, as she eyed the front booth. She wished she'd allowed herself extra time to prepare. She felt more tense than usual, and there was also the fact that the only unpacked, unwrinkled outfit was the same one she'd worn last Friday. Adjusting the scarf at her neck, she questioned just how lucky it truly was. It hadn't worked Friday. Why did she think it would now?

"Your man just got here," Gus said, cutting into her jitters. "Still time to rescue him before Dwayne puts him to sleep." He chuckled and shook his head. "I'll be right over and take your order. Knock him dead, lassie."

Carrie rolled her eyes and forced a smile. "Thanks, Gus."

As she approached the corner Dwayne lifted his chin a notch and looked as if he were about to consummate the sale of the century. He may be a little odd, but she liked him. She couldn't help but smile at him as she neared the booth.

"Carrie, I'm so glad you could join us."

Carrie turned toward her prospective boss, who stood to greet her. "You!"

"Yes, *me*," he said, the contempt in his voice apparent.

All Carrie could do was stare at him.

Dwayne cleared his throat. "Well . . . it appears we may have a minor problem here." He rubbed his hands together, then clasped them to his chest. "But surely nothing that can't be fixed."

Cunningham glared at her as if looks could kill. "I'm afraid there's way too much to fix, the least of which is the front end of my car . . . thanks to this reckless—"

"*Your* car!" The audacity of the man! "Do you know how long I'll have to wait for Woodie's parts?"

"Not as long as you'll have to wait to get a job at Cunningham Construction."

Dwayne clapped his hands together twice, loud and sharp, and they both stared at him, stunned into silence. "Now stop it. Both of you. And sit down. You're acting like children."

"Here we go," Gus said, with forced gusto. "Some of California's finest, on the house."

Carrie looked at Gus's desperate-looking smile and knew her freckles had disappeared behind her scarlet cheeks.

"Well . . . enjoy!" Gus said and raced off.

She braved another peek at Dwayne, who was sharing a stern look between his two mismatched clients as they reluctantly slid into the seats across from him.

"Okay," he started. "We're going to begin again." He took a slow, deliberate sip of Perrier, wiped his mouth with an embroidered handkerchief and then proceeded.

"Carrie Sargent, I'd like you to meet Cash Cunningham. Cash...you may shake her hand and say something polite."

Carrie turned toward Cash, her hand making the long journey from her lap. When she saw his hand slowly rise to meet hers, she let her gaze travel to his face. She caught a slight quiver at the corners of his mouth, and she lost it. She laughed aloud as she clasped his long, elegant fingers. She watched him struggle a second longer before he gave in to his own amusement. She doubted anyone quite like Dwayne had ever crossed this man's path. The idea of anyone scolding this...this... His hand was still in hers as he laughed and eyed Dwayne. Damned if Cash Cunningham weren't one of the most handsome men she'd ever met.

"Now, that's better," Dwayne said, and Carrie withdrew her hand quickly. "We'll just put aside the past and move forward."

He turned to Carrie first. "Carrie, maybe you would like to explain to Cash why you are no longer employed at S & S Construction. Yes. I think that would be a good starting point." He folded his arms and waited.

Carrie turned in her seat and met Cash's gaze. Those eyes. She remembered noticing how blue they were before. Distracted, she answered the question. "My father had a stroke last year. He owned the company I worked for so...so..." Damn, but this was difficult. She tried again. "So when someone made a good offer to buy S & S, we sold it and my father retired. The new owners had their own management team..."

Dwayne finished for her. "So here she is, working temporarily for a friend of the family until we find her something suitable."

Now he turned toward Cash. "Cash, I'd like you to tell Carrie about Cunningham Construction and the position you would like to fill." As before, he leaned back and folded his arms, fully expecting Cash to comply.

Which he did. Carrie listened carefully, surprised at her sudden interest in the job. As Dwayne had told her earlier, it was everything she wanted. Then why, apart from their disastrous first meeting, was she so apprehensive? Maybe it was his too-good looks. Brian had been handsome, and wealthy, too. Yet something told her that was where the resemblance ended, that Cash Cunningham was nothing like her ex-fiancé. But then, her judgment regarding men left something to be desired.

"There," Dwayne said, bringing Carrie back to the present. "That wasn't so difficult." He opened his planner and held his pen in ready. "Cash, when may we schedule another interview? Perhaps at your office?"

Cash twisted his wineglass in his hands and swiped at the condensation. "Why don't I get back to you on that. I'll have to check my calendar."

Dwayne looked crushed, but put up a brave front. "Very well. I'll call you tomorrow and we can discuss it then." He slid out from the booth and Carrie followed suit, Cash right behind her.

Carrie held out her hand to Dwayne. "Thank you, Dwayne. I appreciate your help."

"My pleasure, Carrie," he said, with another limp shake.

She turned to face Cash, not certain what to say. As much as another interview would have been encouraging, she felt a measure of relief at having been politely put off. Before she could speak, he took her hand between both of his. He didn't shake it, but held it there gently. It was something far more intimate than she would have expected from this button-down executive type.

"It's . . . well, it's been interesting, Ms. Sargent." A smile lingering on his lips, he turned and left, his hand now on Dwayne's shoulder, nudging him out the door.

She stood there a moment longer, staring after them. Cash wasn't going to call her back; she knew that. There were other jobs. She'd find something else in time.

So why did his rejection feel like a sharp jab to the solar plexus?

"What do you mean Sam's not here?" Cash lowered his voice and tried again. It wasn't Peg's fault things were in chaos. "Did you try the yard?"

"Yes, sir. Uh—" she swallowed hard, then finished in a flurry " —his wife just called. He's sick and won't be in today."

"Again? How many times does that make this month?" Peg started for the file cabinet and Cash stopped her. "Never mind, Peg. I'll look into it later. For now, why don't you try to find Flutie for me? We need to talk."

The phone rang and Peg darted back to her desk.

"Good morning, Cunningham Construction."

"Good morning, Peg. Dwayne Flutie here."

"Mr. Flutie! I was just about to call you. Just a moment and I'll transfer you right to Mr. Cunningham."

With a blueprint propped open with his elbow, Cash picked up the receiver and barked a greeting. "Hello?"

"Cash...Peg tells me you wanted to talk. Could this have anything to do with last night's meeting in Carmel?"

Cash could hear the dollar signs in Flutie's tone and mentally calculated how much this decision was going to cost him. He sighed out his answer. "Yes, it does. Why don't you give her a call and see if we can talk before the lunch crowd arrives? Tell her I can be there by eleven."

"Wouldn't you rather she come to your office?"

He didn't have time to wait for her day off, whenever that might be. If he made an offer, she'd probably have to give notice at the pub. "No. I'd rather go there . . . as soon as possible." There was a moment of silence at the other end of the line. "Is there a problem?"

"Well . . . actually, I have a luncheon appointment I can't break at this short notice."

Ah, gee. That's too bad. "Look . . . Dwayne . . ." He swallowed a smirk and forced his voice to remain even. "I promise to behave myself in your absence. And by the way, you were right. She does seem to be the perfect person for the job.''

"Thank you, Cash." Another pause, then, "You know, I should be the one to discuss her compensation package with her, should you get that far."

So you can hold me up for the highest possible salary and a higher commission. "Yes, I know." He purposely avoided answering the question, giving his own directive instead. "Give her a call and let Peg know, okay?"

"I'll get right on it."

Cash eyed the blueprint in front of him, then checked his watch. If he left now, he could visit at least one job site and still make it to the pub on time. He rolled up the blueprint, shoved it into its labeled tube and grabbed his briefcase.

As he passed Peg's desk, he called over his shoulder, "Flutie's going to be calling me back. Catch me on the mobile with his answer. I'll be back after two, Peg."

Peg waved an acknowledgment and picked up the next call.

Carrie replaced the receiver and met Gus's curious gaze.

"Cunningham wants to talk with me . . . here at eleven."

"How 'bout that! He's not as pigheaded as I thought he was," Gus said with a devilish twinkle in his eye. "I think you have a new job, lass."

A part of her said Gus was right. Another part left her breathless and worried. But there wasn't time to analyze why. Tables needed setup and the bar needed restocking. She pulled a couple of fifths from the crate, wiped them with a damp cloth and found empty spaces behind Gus. "Even if he makes an offer—which isn't at all a sure thing— I'll still give you two weeks' notice."

Gus stopped wiping the counter and faced her. "You'll do no such thing, Carrie Sargent. If he wants you to start tomorrow, you go."

"But you've already scheduled—"

He gripped her by the shoulders and finished her sentence. "I've already scheduled you for more hours than two of my regulars... which means they're grousing among themselves when they know I'm listening. So it's settled, lass."

"Why didn't you tell me, Gus?" She'd half suspected as much from her lukewarm treatment by the other waitresses, but she'd hoped it was just because she was new and had to prove herself.

"Because I knew you'd find something soon and they'd get over it. Besides, the same ones complain when I don't give 'em enough time off. So now, Carrie darlin', do we have a deal?"

She pulled him into a bear hug. "You're not the crusty old goat you pretend to be, Gus McGee," she said, a sheen settling over her eyes.

He thumped her on the back and returned to his chores, disguising his own emotions with a gruff response. "Well, we'll see about that. If ya don't get those tables ready before I open the door, I might have to fire ya before ya ever set eyes on that Mr. Cunningham."

She threw a stack of napkins atop a tray of silverware and rushed around the end of the bar, doing her best to feign fear at his idle threat.

Her tasks were barely complete when Gus unlocked the door at 10:30 and a stream of patrons rushed in. Carrie greeted them all with a smile, calling the regulars by name as she ushered them to a booth or table. It was nearly eleven before more help arrived and the customers' needs were all attended to. She'd intentionally left the front booth by the window unoccupied. Now she noticed the lone figure there. He'd seated himself and was patiently waiting, watching her every move. Dark hair and blue eyes faced her whenever she stole a peek.

Finally Gus took her tray and whispered near her ear, "What are you waiting for? Christmas? Go talk to the man, lass. We got things covered."

Carrie wiped her hands on her apron and tucked unruly curls behind each ear, exhaled a long breath and walked to the corner booth. She slid in opposite him, noticing her shortness of breath—which seemed to be a recurring problem whenever she was near this man. Was she intimidated or bedazzled? Either way, she didn't like it, and she fought for a measure of control.

"Would you like some coffee?" *Way to go. Start off subservient. That strengthens your position.*

"No, thanks. I've had my fill for the day." His planner was open to blank note pages, with his pen resting on top. "Are you sure you can spare the time now? I don't want to cause you trouble on the job."

Well, I'll be! Sensitivity. Maybe she'd misjudged him. "It's okay. I told Gus you were coming and he said to take whatever time we need."

Cash picked up his pen and rolled it in those long, elegant fingers of his—fingers she could picture on a keyboard, rather than a high beam on a construction site. Slow, methodical fingers. She forced her gaze away from his hands. It wasn't calming her nerves in the least. He raised his head and eyed her, seeming to weigh his words carefully before he spoke.

"Your résumé is impressive and your references think highly of you."

But? She could feel his hesitation.

"Are you interested in the job?"

She blinked twice, trying not to let her mouth fall open. "Well . . . yes, I am." She straightened in her seat. "Is this the time to discuss terms?"

He smiled, then thumbed through his planner for a page of prepared figures, which he tore out and placed on the table. Slowly he turned the page around and slid it closer to her, nodding for her to read.

After one full year—insurance and one week's vacation. He had to be kidding. She glanced up, hoping to find a teasing smile, but was met by a poker face. She looked back to the paper and skimmed to the last line—compensation.

That did it!

"You can't be serious?" She shoved the paper back in his direction.

His jaw muscles tightened. "You don't like the terms?"

"Terms?" She tried to control her temper, but felt it slipping by degrees. "Those aren't terms."

"And what would *you* call them?" His anger flared as easily as hers.

"I'd call them a cash-and-carry discount plan! That's what I'd call them."

His anger disappeared, replaced by an amused smirk. "Cash and Carrie." He paused a moment, considering her words, then laughed a low laugh and shook his head. "We're bound to be the brunt of a few jokes around the office. Never thought of that before." Then he met her gaze again. "Okay. I give, *Carrie*." He leaned on her name. "What do you think would be fair?"

Carrie relaxed a little, encouraged by his reaction. Anyone with a sense of humor couldn't be all bad. "First tell me what your policy manual says about insurance and vacation. You can't very well give me something contrary to the manual."

Cash closed his planner, leaned back and crossed his arms. His gaze drifted around the room before settling on hers.

"You don't have a policy manual?" she asked incredulously.

"Have you ever written one?"

"Yes."

"Then maybe that should be your first task. Are you up to the challenge?" He shot her a coy look, and she picked up his pen.

Retrieving the paper, she scribbled new terms next to his, then slid it back to him. "Are you up to these?" He drummed his fingers in silence, and she thought she'd pushed too far.

Finally he folded the paper, stuffed it in the back pocket of his planner and slid from the booth. Carrie sat looking up at him, her stomach in her throat once again.

"Do you have to give notice?"

She exhaled softly. "No."

"Will eight tomorrow morning work for you?"

She slid from the booth, her feet now inches from his. She put on her best piece-of-cake smile and pretended not to notice his baby blues gazing down at her. "Eight tomorrow it is."

Four

Early Wednesday morning Gus pulled up at the front door. Carrie yawned, then stretched across the car's console, planting a kiss on his unshaved cheek. "What would I do without you, Gus McGee?"

He waved his hand as though it were no big deal. "What time should I pick ya up, lass?"

"Uh-uh. You take care of happy hour, and I'll manage on my own." She opened her door and stepped out, the wind catching her wild mane. With one hand on the door and the other pushing back a heavily moussed tangle of curls, she gave him one last nervous smile. "Thanks, Gus. I'll tell you all about it tonight."

"Okay, lass, but if ya find ya need a ride, ya call."

She shut the door, made a small X over her breast pocket, then waved over her shoulder as she fought a bone-chilling wind the last dozen yards to the entrance.

This weather was just the wake-up call she needed. She'd helped close the pub at 2:00 a.m., then tossed and turned till the alarm sounded at six. Now, as Carrie strode through the front door of Cunningham Construction, butterflies flickered behind her ribcage and a small laugh passed her lips. The last time she walked out that door, she'd been certain she'd never return.

She punched the elevator button and studied the barren atrium with more interest than the first time. It was a massive space that begged for warmth. Maybe everything had been cleared out in anticipation of the holidays. She could picture a tall pine with all the trimmings and large red poinsettias here and there. The door slid open and she stepped in. She smoothed the wrinkles from her navy skirt and straightened the red-white-and-blue scarf that had been tied in a large, loose bow just above the lapels of her red blazer. When she stepped out a moment later, Peggy came around the reception desk and offered her hand.

"Ms. Sargent . . . welcome! I'm so glad you got the job." Her handshake was firm and energetic. Carrie smiled back, knowing she'd already made her first friend at Cunningham Construction.

"Thank you, Peggy. I'm glad to be here. But why don't you call me Carrie? I'm not big on formalities."

Peggy pumped her hand again, excitedly. "Okay . . . Carrie. I can't tell you how happy I am that we're getting some help around here . . . especially someone with all your experience." She finally let go of Carrie's hand when the phone rang.

Carrie watched the young woman as she answered the phone. There was a smile in her voice, as well as on her face. Cash was lucky to find this one, she decided, just as she saw him round the corner.

"Ms. Sargent! Welcome aboard." He closed the space between them and extended his hand. She gripped it in hers, remembering the first time he'd taken her hand in both of his. She shook it quickly and let go, an uneasy feeling spreading through her. Poise. Confidence. Where were they when she needed them? Somehow she found her voice.

"Do you mind calling me Carrie?"

"If that's what you'd like," he said, and she noticed him giving her a quick once-over. She did look a little like an American flag, but a clean, crisp American flag. Maybe she should go stand in the atrium and brighten things up.

"So... Cash... where do I begin?"

He arched an eyebrow and she knew her mistake instantly. *Cash*. He hadn't asked her to call him by *his* first name. Oh, for Pete's sake. This was a construction company, not the UN. She continued to smile at him as if she didn't have a clue his feathers had been ruffled.

Finally he turned around and said, "Follow me."

His pace was brisk, no-nonsense. She had trouble keeping up. They passed his open door and he turned into the next room, stopping abruptly, with Carrie right on his heels. Somehow she managed to keep from running into him, but when he turned to face her she was close enough to feel his long sigh on her forehead. She stepped back and pretended to take in the room, avoiding those damnable blue eyes.

"This will be your office," he said, getting right down to brass tacks.

When she finally did look, she saw an eight-foot walnut-veneer folding table in the center, surrounded by eight armless brown vinyl chairs. And nothing else. She didn't know what she'd expected, but this wasn't it, not in a building as grand as this one.

The carpet was commercial brown tweed. A large glass wall was covered with off-white vertical blinds, the same shade as the flat-painted walls. There had to be a redeeming quality, if she looked hard enough. In her mind's eye she pictured her first visit. If her memory was right, behind the closed blinds should be a view of the Pacific. With a little work...

"This used to be a conference room," Cash said, forestalling her decorating ideas. "I never use it anymore, since there's a larger one with a wet bar in the new wing. Besides, I thought we may find it convenient to be next door to each other." For some reason he suddenly seemed uncomfortable, but he pushed on. "I've ordered a phone, which should be installed Monday. As to the rest, make a list of what you think you'll need and we'll talk about it. For now, I'll take you down to Purchasing and Fran will set you up with basic supplies."

He started to go and she followed. "And my computer?" she said to his back. He stopped dead in his tracks, and she almost ran into him again. *Damn!* She wished he'd stop doing that. He turned sideways and eyed her as if she'd just poked a gun in his back.

"Computer?"

"Well, yes. The employee handbook is a very long and arduous project—even with a word processor. And I'll need desktop publishing for all the related forms. Then I was thinking there would be a company newsletter, and memos for special events... some graphics software would be nice for that—"

Cash held up both hands. "Whoa, slow down. We'll get you some paper and pencils, stapler, that kind of stuff. Then we'll see about the rest."

She saw him roll his eyes as he turned and started off again.

"Of course, I'll need a desk and an ergonomic chair..."

His head tilted back and he stared at the ceiling, the set of his shoulders telling her he was ready to blow a gasket, but he kept moving. Along the way she noticed work areas separated by free-standing beige partitions. Still no plants, no family photos, no doodads. Unsmiling people hunched over their work, only a few giving her passing notice. The more she saw, the more she knew her first impression of this guy had been right—a self-centered, arrogant iceman. A nice outer package with nothing inside.

When they reached the purchasing department, a middle-aged woman with short gray hair swiveled away from her computer and eyed them curiously. Thank God, a computer! At least he believed in modern technology, Carrie thought as Cash half turned for introductions.

"Fran Wilson, I'd like you to meet Carrie Sargent, our new Human Resources Manager."

Fran stayed seated and peered over her half-glasses. "Nice to meet you," she said with cool efficiency.

"Carrie..." His gaze met hers briefly, then flitted away. "I'm going to leave you with Fran. She'll introduce you around and get your supplies." He glanced at his watch. "I have an appointment, but I'll be back just before noon. If you don't mind working over lunch, we could discuss that list of needs of yours and prioritize a few assignments." Now he held her steady gaze and awaited a reply.

"F-fine," she stammered, not sure why she was still here. Flutie had made a big mistake if he thought she could work for this man.

He left her staring after him. She forced her gaze away from the doorway and back to Fran, who seemed to be scrutinizing the new kid's hair and wardrobe. Fran wore a smart gray knit suit the color of her hair, which meant she was in perfect harmony with her drab surroundings.

Ah, a plethora of challenges. Well, S, if you're going to stay, there's no time like the present to meet one of them head-on.

Carrie took a seat in front of Fran's desk and heaved a sigh. Leaning closer on her elbow, she looked the woman in the eye, smiled and said, "So, Fran...do you have any pets?"

Three hours later Cash jogged up the back stairway and went directly to Carrie's office, wondering if he'd made a mistake in planning lunch with her the very first day. Surely she'd have more questions later, but by then he'd be out of town. Besides, there was no better time than day one to let her know his employees call him "Mr. Cunningham" and that she'd have to tone down her flamboyant attire.

He pushed a stray hair off his forehead and straightened his tie as he neared her office, never slowing his pace till he crossed her threshold, then he nearly staggered backward. Gone were the folding table and chairs. In their place sat an old oak desk, a typing stand perpendicular to one side, with Carrie pecking away at a computer keyboard atop it. *What the—?*

"Cash! Isn't this great?" She gestured with a sweep of her arm. "Fran and I found the desk under a tarp in the shop. We had to move a lot of boxes off it and clean it up, but I love it. Much better than any new thing. The guys in the shop were real sweet and carried it up here. And look at this." She turned her palm up toward the computer. "Fran said it's just been gathering dust in the storage room since she got her new one."

With hands on hips, Cash took it all in. It didn't have the crisp contemporary feel everything else did, but the price was right.

"I'll need a new chair, though," she said, her fingers back at the keyboard, doing who knew what. A person would think she'd been here forever.

She looked up from her work. "Is it time for lunch yet? I could eat the back end of a skunk I'm so hungry."

He knew his mouth had dropped open, but he found it difficult to either move or speak.

"Oh, I forgot. You'll probably want to look at your messages first," she said, pounding away at the computer.

"Uh . . . right." He managed to find his voice. "Just give me a minute." He walked to his office, feeling as though he'd stepped into some time warp, and this was his first day on the job instead of hers.

The feeling lingered on the short drive to Fish Hopper's and all through lunch as he listened to her ideas for—he had to remind himself—*his* company.

When she took a breath and drank some iced tea, Cash seized the first quiet moment. "I'm glad you've started on the new policy manual, but there's something else I'd like you to think about.'' She set her glass down and waited. *Well, what do you know? She can keep her mouth shut.*

"There's been a higher-than-usual amount of turnover and absenteeism lately. Morale seems a little low, too." Carrie smiled and leaned forward, resting her elbows on the table, looking as though he'd just offered her dessert instead of a challenge. "Maybe you could come up with a few ideas to help turn things around.'' She seemed to vibrate with enthusiasm, as if she might overflow any moment if he didn't let her speak. He leaned back in his chair and watched her green eyes widen as she took a deep breath and began.

"I have a couple ideas already."

Surprise, surprise.

"But will you excuse me a minute? Have to go check out the plumbing.'' She started to leave the table, then whispered near his ear, "My dad's company actually *did* the plumbing here, you know."

"No! Really?" He could picture a fleet of work vans with happy-face toilets painted on the sides.

She smiled and gave a proud nod before swinging her hair around and heading toward the restrooms.

Through the tinted window Cash watched a sea lion struggle to top a boulder that rose above shallow waters. Each time he tried, a wave would take him back out. With another valiant effort he shimmied higher, finally flopping over on his back, looking exhausted as he prepared for a nap. He knew just how the guy felt, Cash thought as Carrie rejoined the table.

She turned in her seat and followed his gaze. "Aren't they adorable?" Then she faced him again. "Do you ever go over to the aquarium and watch the otters? I love the way they groom themselves with their little hands. Kind of like raccoons, don't you think?"

Cash leaned forward and rested his elbows on the table, steepling his fingers and trying his hardest to get the conversation back on track. "I've never been to the aquarium and I've never given much thought to sea otters. Now about—''

''You've never been to the aquarium? Oh, Cash, you don't know what you're missing. Monterey has one of the biggest and best in the world. Some of the tanks are thirty feet high...with sharks in them! You know—'' she glanced over her shoulder at the sea lion, then back to Cash ''—it would be great to have a Saturday or Sunday outing for all the employees at the aquarium.... They could bring their families, too.'' She slapped the table, seeming proud of herself. ''Yep. Just what you need to boost morale.''

Cash lifted his arm and stared at his watch. Thank God it was time to leave. Just wait till the next time he ran into Flutie. How could that man possibly think she would last at a company like Cunningham?

He picked up the check and calculated fifteen percent. Standing, he extracted two singles from his wallet, then dug in his pocket for change and counted out the thirty-six cents he needed. When he placed the tip on the table, he noticed Carrie eyeing him from the side of her face.

''Come on.... We'll talk more about your...ideas...in the car,'' he said, escorting her out.

All the way back to the office, Carrie talked nonstop. She never seemed to falter in her positive attitude and her firm belief that her ideas could solve any problem.

She sprang from her side of the car as soon as they parked and came alongside him. ''So what do you think?'' she asked.

He *thought* he had a headache. The fact that he'd be out of town on job sites for the next week only marginally relieved the throbbing in his temples. He should have nipped this thing in the bud. Now he'd have to wait till he got back. He stepped up his pace to the front door and tried to convey his shortness of time, if not patience. She practically ran to keep up.

''Okay,'' he conceded. ''Your intercompany newsletter idea sounds fine.'' And less expensive than some of the other things. "And you can order a new chair." Whoever replaced her would need one anyway. He opened the door and let her precede him. "Is there anything else for now?" Once inside, he brushed past her and punched the elevator button. She caught up as the door slid open and they stepped in.

"Just one more thing."

Exasperated, he shot her an impatient glance, and she finished quickly.

"About those morale boosters. There're a couple of little things I could do while you're gone that could show immediate results. Nothing extravagant."

She was looking up at him with those adorable green eyes, reminding him of a little girl pleading for a pony ride. With eyes like those, she'd probably gotten away with her outrageous behavior all her life. It occurred to him to ask exactly how much these "couple of little things" were going to cost him, but then he'd be late for his next appointment while she enumerated the endless details.

The door slid open and he strode toward his office, grabbing a stack of messages off Peggy's desk as he passed. Carrie was right on his heels. At his doorway he stopped and faced her, making it clear that he had other things to do and she wasn't invited in.

"Okay. Try a few things." He watched her face light up, and he couldn't help but smile. "But be conservative with the spending, okay?" He didn't wait for an answer, but instead walked to his chair and turned his attention to the messages in his hand.

"Thanks, Cash," he heard her say, halfway to her own office.

He dropped the notes on his desk. *Damn.* He'd meant to tell her not to call him that. And her clothes...

He rocked back in his chair and clasped his hands behind his aching head. *Oh, my God! I've hired a hurricane... and let her loose in my nice, neat, orderly world.*

He cracked his neck from side to side trying to alleviate the tension. Maybe he should have been more specific when he told her to keep the spending conservative. Then again, she'd seemed happy with that old desk and computer. *Nah.* The new employee manual would keep her occupied. He had other things to worry about right now. Next week was soon enough to decide what to do with his new employee.

He picked up the first message and swiveled to the window, phone nestled at his neck. He was getting all worked up over nothing.

Besides . . . how much damage could she do in just one short week?

Five

―――――

"Gus? Am I calling at a bad time?" Carrie hiked her right shoulder to the receiver and lifted a pen and paper from Fran's desk.

"Nope. Just finished restocking the bar... Ten minutes till I open the door. Everything goin' okay, lass?"

"Hunky-dory. I just called to get a name and phone number from you. Do you have a business card or receipt or something from that T-shirt place you use for the pub?"

"Hold on. I think I know where I put it." She heard the phone clunk against the counter and she smiled, picturing the old place. In a way she missed working at Day's, but this job was right up her alley. Challenges galore. Besides, she had dinner at Day's most nights and still lived upstairs.

"Here it is," Gus said, huffing into the phone. "Got a pencil?"

"Yep. Shoot." She wrote out the name and phone number, then made plans for a late dinner with him. When she hung up, Fran was eyeing her, an obvious question on the tip of her tongue.

"Boyfriend?" she asked shyly, acting as though she knew it was none of her business.

Carrie laughed and shook her head. "No, no. Gus is my father's best friend . . . kind of my surrogate dad since mine went back east. I rent an apartment above his pub." Fran's eyebrows shot up, concern on her wrinkled brow. "It's a very nice pub, actually." Then the idea came to her. "Fran! Why don't you join us for dinner tonight?"

Her hand flew to her chest. "Oh, no. I couldn't intrude."

She was dying to go, and Carrie could see it in the lonely widow's face. "It won't be an intrusion at all. You'd be doing me a favor, since I need a ride home anyway."

Fran smoothed back her perfectly coiffed hair. "Well, if you need a ride—"

"Great! It's settled then. Unless there's a problem with Fefe . . ."

"Oh, no. I go shopping or to movies some nights, and she's perfectly content to snuggle on the sofa and sleep while I'm gone." She frowned and thought a moment. "Maybe we should stop by and let her go out to do her business, though."

"No problem. Then I can meet Fefe in person." Carrie smiled, pecking her finger at the picture Fran had brought in to show off her toy poodle. "Now . . . about those T-shirts . . ."

Another hour and they put down the employee list with a sigh. They'd done their best to guess how many smalls, mediums, larges and extra larges. Now they were debating color and style.

"The knit shirts with collars are nice, don't you think?" Carrie looked up from the catalog to Fran's small face. She pushed her glasses a notch higher on her nose, then glanced at Carrie before pointing to the price.

"The T-shirts would be several hundred dollars less . . . with as many as we have to order." She shot Carrie a worried "Know what I mean?" look.

"Ah, yes. We'll have to order some extra, too, in case somebody needs a different size and for future employees. T-shirts it is. Now what about color?"

"The dark teal with mauve lettering is very attractive," Fran said, looking at the chart.

"Hmm . . . Yes, it is. But do you think the macho men in the field and shop would like it?"

"I see your point. How about this?" She pointed to a burgundy shirt with a hunter-green logo.

"Ooh. I like that. And with the holidays coming, won't it look great on everyone . . . with all the red and green decorations?" Carrie watched Fran purse her lips and drop her chin. "What? Did I say something wrong?"

Fran fidgeted with the corner of the page and avoided eye contact. "No . . . it's just that . . . well, Mr. Cunningham doesn't decorate for the holidays."

"You're kidding?" She wasn't, by the look on her face. "Well, we'll just have to see about that, won't we?" Carrie winked, and the older woman's mouth curved upward in a conspiratorial grin.

"You don't mean to say—"

"Oh, yes. That's exactly what I mean to say." They shared a silent moment, imagining the shock on Cash's face when he returned. Suddenly Carrie sprang out of her chair. "You call in the T-shirt order and I'll go talk to the guys in the yard. They must be clearing at least one job site that has a big pine tree on it."

With a reassuring pat to Fran's hand Carrie strode off, devilish excitement pulsing through her veins. It was only Thursday, and Cash wouldn't be back till next Wednesday afternoon—the day before Thanksgiving. Perfect. He said she could try a few morale boosters. What better way to bring about a few smiles than decorating a Christmas tree?

Oh, and of course there was the matter of family photos and plants in each employee's work space....

It was all she could do to keep from skipping down the hall. She could see the happy faces already. The first newsletter would go out tomorrow, along with paychecks. In it they'd read her suggestions. Yesiree, Bob, by Wednesday afternoon this place would be humming.

Wednesday afternoon Cash stood the collar up on his trench coat and leaned into the biting wind as he made his way to the back door. Just inside, he checked the second hand on his wristwatch, then jogged up the emergency stairwell. At the top of the third floor he looked at his watch again and calculated the time. *Damn.* Ten seconds slower than last week. He was getting soft. Time for a good workout at the gym.

He took off his coat and folded it over his arm as he strolled down the hall to his office, humming along with the Christmas carol that was playing over the—

He stopped in the middle of the hall and listened. The soft instrumental sounds came from everywhere. He'd never used the sound system except to page someone. Was it a radio or tape? But more important, where had one come from, since the company had never owned either? It took only a heartbeat to figure out who was behind this. Well, he'd just have to set things straight with Ms. Sargent.

With each long stride, the music swelled in his head and he remembered earlier Christmases, times when the sounds of loud singing and bawdy jokes roused him from his boyhood dreams, when glasses were flung into the fireplace amid gales of drunken laughter.

By the time he'd approached Carrie's office, he'd worked up a good head of steam. How could anyone get a honest day's work done with music playing? He rounded her corner ready to do battle but the office was empty. Well, not exactly empty. She wasn't there, but a large potted ficus stood in front of the glass wall, the blinds pulled completely open. A framed portrait of Carrie with her father hung on an adjacent wall. *So she's made herself right at home, has she?* Not for long. Hadn't she noticed there were no personal effects in the other employees' areas? If she had, did she think it coincidental?

He stood in the doorway and pushed his suit coat back with his balled fists, wondering where the loose cannon he'd hired was hiding . . . and why he'd ever hired her in the first place. God knew there'd been enough warning signs that spelled *Trouble*.

He stalked to his own office, threw his top coat over a side chair and went in search of Trouble. It shouldn't be hard to find all that red hair, not to mention she never shut up. He could hardly wait to see what kind of getup she had on today. He wondered if she even owned a simple navy or gray suit.

He started with Peggy, but she wasn't at her desk, either. He noticed the answering system had been switched on. At three o'clock in the afternoon? Now whose idea was that? He raked his hair with his fingers and nodded his head. Stupid question.

He headed for Fran's desk. Certainly she'd know what was going on.

But when he got there, instead of Fran, he found an ornately framed photo of a pompadoured gray poodle next to a flowing English ivy that cascaded to the floor. Pivoting in the aisle, he saw more of the same on other desks. One short week and the place looked like some great-grandmother's parlor. Plants and photos, plants and photos . . .

He heard laughter and voices from somewhere and stopped to listen. They were coming from the atrium. A moment later he was back at the elevator, punching the button for the third time. He was tempted to take the stairs when the door finally opened. He rode to the lobby, seething. Didn't anybody believe in work around here? He'd been out of town many times before, and nothing like this had ever happened. He would have thought his old-timers would... The elevator opened, and the music he'd heard earlier grew louder, along with laughter and the shuffling of boxes, tinkling of...

He bounded out and came to a dead stop. Hands on hips, he stared at the atrium in front of him, not believing what his eyes told him. Dozens of busy little elves dressed in burgundy-and-green T-shirts darted around in front of a tree that towered at least twenty feet above them. Tall ladders had been erected on all sides, with employees perched near the top leaning into the tree. Bulbs were being handed to them from a chain of hands stationed on lower rungs and the floor below.

Mouth agape, Cash took a tentative step forward and read the back of a shirt. Cunningham Construction, Monterey, California. Across the room he caught a front view of another. Two dark green blocked Cs mirrored each other, forming a broken circle. In the center of the circle stood a lone cypress, the symbol of Monterey. *Well, well. At least my logo hasn't changed since I left.* He had to admit the shirts were in good taste and that—

One of his men spotted him and closed the distance between them, reaching for Cash's hand when he drew near. "Thanks, Mr. Cunningham. This is the best afternoon I ever spent here." He pumped Cash's hand vigorously. "Thanks again, boss." Cash did his best to smile, not sure his mouth registered the sentiment.

Then he saw Fran working her way toward him, and the word *traitor* sounded in the back of his head. Fran had always been his loyal watchdog. How could she have let this happen in his absence? He narrowed his eyes as she approached, letting her know she was in for a tongue-lashing. But when she stopped in front of him, his gaze traveled the length of her and he forgot what he meant to say. She wore hunter-green corduroy pants. He couldn't remember ever seeing Fran in anything other than a skirt. He was surprised she even owned such a thing.

"Do you like them?" she asked demurely. "I bought them to go with the new shirt."

Cash began to answer, but then Sam, his shop foreman, raced up. "Boss! Happy Thanksgiving. And thanks for all this." He pointed to his T-shirt with one hand and gestured to the tree with the other. Just as quickly, he turned back to the crowd, calling a last thought over his shoulder. "That Carrie is something else, isn't she?"

She sure is. Was that liquor he'd smelled on Sam's breath, or was the strong scent of pine deceiving his senses? He scanned the area again, not seeing evidence of refreshments, and still not seeing that familiar head of copper curls. He turned back to Fran, but she was gone. Suddenly the voices all around him rose up as one. A boisterous verse of "Jingle Bells" drowned out the music coming over the sound system.

And then he spotted her.

Her legs held firmly in place by Peg, Carrie stretched out on the top rung of a ladder, giving him a too-vivid view of her formfitting jeans. She stretched a little farther and he held his breath. As she secured a large star atop the massive pine, a loud cheer went up from the crowd and she turned her beaming face to them. Cash watched as her gaze swept lovingly over her merry elves. She smiled from ear to ear while adjusting the large red Santa cap tilted on her head.

Good God, he'd hired Christmas Carol! What on earth had possessed him—?

"Cash!" She waved her arm above her head, and the crowd turned toward him in unison.

"Isn't it beautiful?" she shouted after the last refrain. Without waiting for his response, she shooed Peg down the ladder and scrambled excitedly behind her. He followed the bouncing red curls as Carrie pressed through the animated crowd and stopped abruptly in front of him.

Breathless, she said, "We were just about to plug in the lights." She turned around and eyed Fran. "I think Cash should do it, don't you?"

Fran shot a nervous glance in his direction, then looked back at Carrie. "If he'd like. Yes, that would be nice."

Carrie turned back to Cash. "Want to?"

Want to *what?* Take her over his knee and spank her? Yes, he wanted to. But then the image took on a different slant and he shifted his weight to the opposite leg. What was it about this woman that made him feel like a visitor to his own business? And what had happened to his directive to keep the spending conservative?

As if reading his thoughts, she leaned in and spoke in a voice intended for his ears only. "The tree was free... from one of the job sites. And they all brought decorations from home. I thought they'd feel like it was theirs that way...and it wouldn't cost anything, either...except for the lights." She was looking up at him with those round green eyes again, beseeching him not to spoil her party.

"And the T-shirts? Who paid for them?" He folded his arms in front of him and looked down his nose at her, trying his hardest to sound stern and disapproving, though somehow he knew she'd win this point, too.

To her credit, she didn't flinch or look away. "Well, we haven't got the bill yet, but I got a discount, since the owner is a friend of Gus's. Besides, I was sure you'd want employees to wear them for casual days."

"Casual days?"

"Yes, you know... one of those morale boosters I asked you about. Well, you see, in the newsletter I told everyone that Fridays would be casual days from now on ... as well as special occasions like today."

Cash cocked his head, demanding more.

"A lot of companies do this now—let employees dress more casually at the end of the week." She wrinkled her forehead and started waving an index finger at him. "But you know... some places have trouble with casual turning into grubby. So if you tell them to wear company logo shirts on casual day and no holey-knee or ragged-cuff jeans, then voilà!" She gestured to the crowd behind her with a sweeping hand, her expression saying only one logical conclusion could be reached—that she'd made the best decision for the company.

Had she? He let his gaze travel behind her to his employees. A hush had fallen over them, and many were staring at their feet, thumbs hooked in back belt loops, waiting for Scrooge to lower the boom.

Ignoring Carrie, he strode directly to Peggy, who held the end of the extension cord in her shaking fingers. Her eyes grew larger with each step he took in her direction. What kind of ogre did these people think he was? Did they expect him to shout, "Bah, humbug"?

He snatched the plug from Peggy and walked to the wall. Positioning the prongs over the outlet, he looked back at the tree, then pushed his hand to the wall. Thousands of tiny white lights danced across long, graceful boughs. A collective sigh echoed through the atrium, followed by a few hesitant claps, then a more hearty round of applause. Looking at the smiling faces around him, Cash smiled back, feeling a bond he'd never thought much about before today. They were the only family he had. He cared about these people. He always had, but there had never been an appropriate way to show it.

"Well? What are you all standing around looking at?" He forced his voice to sound tough, hoping that would stem the flow of unwanted emotions that pushed behind his ribs. "Go on home to your families." He flicked his wrist toward the front door. "Happy Thanksgiving," he said in a husky tone, then turned and headed for the elevator, avoiding all eyes.

Before he reached the elevator, a chorus of "For He's a Jolly Good Fellow" sprang up behind him. He stepped into the elevator without looking back. The door slid shut as moisture blurred his vision and a vise tightened its grip around his throat.

When he dropped into his chair a moment later, he swiveled to the glass wall behind him. He hiked one hip and extracted a handkerchief from his back pocket, dabbed at his eyes and finally blew his nose. He stared at the whitecaps far below. The sea looked cold and turbulent, just about the way he felt . . . or usually felt.

This was a place of business, not some social hall. He'd been wise to keep his distance from his employees all these years. It was the only way to command respect.

Wasn't it?

Yes, he told himself. It was.

Maybe if his father had kept his mind on business instead of his wife's continuous partying, they'd both be here today. He watched another wave explode against a pile of rocks and remembered another angry sea, a time when the shore had seemed miles away, his arms screaming with pain, the current so strong he was sure—

The soft knock on the open door brought him around with a start.

"Cash? Do you have a minute?"

The glare from the glass behind him blinded him, but there was no mistaking the voice. He blinked and she came into view.

"What is it?" He hadn't meant to sound so gruff, but, damn! Would that woman ever give him a moment's peace? With a sigh he pointed to the chair in front of his desk and she sat in it, looking nervous and contrite.

"First, I wanted to explain about the shirts," she began hesitantly.

He rocked back in his chair and waited, giving her nothing to ease her discomfort. After all, she'd spent an enormous amount of money without consulting him first.

"In the newsletter I explained that the company would buy the original one and that extras could be purchased through payroll deduction. So this is a onetime expense and—"

"They look very nice." Now why had he said that? He had her on the run.

She smiled and sat back in her chair, her relief obvious. "Thank you. Actually, Fran picked them out." Carrie played with a fingernail, then braved another glance. "The logo is beautiful. I thought it came out real nice."

"Yes. Yes, it did." He watched her eyes brighten as she leaned forward, her elbow now on the edge of his desk.

Cash moved closer, too, and propped a cheek on his right fist. At this distance he could see flecks of yellow mixed with the green. Her long lashes were thick and darker than—

"I was thinking about coming in Friday. With no one here I should be able to finish the first draft of the employee manual. But..."

She lowered her eyes and he noticed a lighter shade of green shadow artfully applied to her lids. He felt himself smiling at her, waiting for her to finish.

"But... well... I don't have a key."

Cash straightened in his chair, effectively breaking his reverie.

A key. A simple little thing but it felt like a giant step— like asking someone to move in after a couple of dates. So why was he opening his center drawer and reaching for one? If he wasn't going to keep her here this was a stupid move. When she left he'd have to change all the locks and...

He handed her a key and she reached out tentatively, her small fingers grazing over his as she withdrew it slowly. He didn't move his hands, but stared at them instead, her touch lingering in his mind as real as her rosy scent in the air between them.

"Do you have plans for tomorrow?" she asked.

Her voice sounded timid to his ears, and for a moment he thought she might ask him to join her for dinner, but when he said, "No. Nothing special," she just looked at him for the longest time without speaking.

Finally she asked, "Will you be here on Friday?"

Disappointed and relieved at the same time, he watched her pocket the key and avert her gaze. "Some part of the day. Yes, I will."

She rose from her chair and turned away. "I'll see you then. Happy Thanksgiving, Cash."

"Happy Thanksgiving, Carrie," he said, but she'd already left the room.

Six

Cash downed the dregs of his coffee and looked at his watch. It was nearly eleven. Maybe she'd changed her mind. He pushed out of his chair and strolled to the break room, taking in the virtual garden that had grown up around each desk. He had to admit it did add warmth to the place. He'd told her that first day that he wanted her help in boosting morale. She certainly had done that.

He finished making a fresh pot and let his mind drift back to Wednesday afternoon. A slow smile crossed his lips as he envisioned Carrie atop the ladder in her Santa cap. He chuckled and refilled his mug. She was something else, all right. If he could just rein her in a little. He pictured the smiling faces around the tree and the handsome new shirts. Was all that time away from work and all the added expense justified? Would the glow continue come Monday and beyond? Time would tell.

He walked back to his office and sat down with a weary thud. His stomach growled, reminding him he hadn't eaten since last night's tuna salad. Some Thanksgiving dinner. He harrumphed and returned to the pile of correspondence on his desk. Halfway through the first page he heard a noise and stopped. It was coming from next door. A rattling of papers, a clinking of... It sounded like glass. He walked to the door and listened again, for a moment hearing nothing. Then there it was again. It didn't sound like paperwork being shuffled or a keyboard at work. If Carrie had come in while he was making coffee, you'd think she'd pop her head in and say hello. He walked to the next office and peered around the door jamb.

"Cash!" She popped up off the floor in the far corner of the room and stood in front of whatever she was hiding. "I... I was going to come get you when I finished...." She motioned behind her, looking embarrassed, a cute pink tinge washing over her freckles.

Curious, he moved closer. What was she up to now? And why did she have to fit so perfectly into those worn, tight jeans? He groaned inwardly, knowing he couldn't very well criticize her attire. After all, it was a day off and she didn't have to be here. He stopped in front of her and waited. One thing was certain. If he remained silent long enough, she'd talk.

"I... I didn't know if you had a traditional dinner yesterday," she began. "Gus and I did the whole shebang."

He smiled at his small victory.

"So I thought maybe we could have some leftovers for lunch." She stepped aside and revealed her efforts. A blanket was spread in the corner, a large picnic basket sitting on it. Paper plates and matching napkins covered with large turkeys sat facing each other. Crystal and silverware completed the settings. "I put it here so we could each have a wall to lean against while we ate."

Cash looked from the blanket to her impish face and her sparkling round green eyes, for a moment forgetting about the food. Quickly he tugged at his pant legs and sat crossed-legged on the floor.

"Well? What are we eating?" He smiled up at her, and her face radiated happiness. A halo of sunshine filtered through her wild hair from the glass wall behind her, and for a moment she looked like an angel. His heart skipped a beat. Then she sat down opposite him and began rummaging through the basket and he regained some control.

Out came one bowl after another, each covered in an insulated pouch. Soon he saw turkey, dressing, mashed potatoes, gravy. There was even a small bowl of whole cranberries and a tossed salad.

When she reached for the bottle of sparkling water, he took it from her, his fingers touching hers, and that strange feeling shot through him, just as it had before. This was no angel. She was the devil in disguise. Right here in the office . . . plying him with food . . . softening him up for . . .

For what?

He opened the bottle and poured. The food looked and smelled heavenly. But Carrie? She looked and smelled like trouble. Even if she was a good employee—and he still wasn't convinced of that—she couldn't be his friend or anything else. Friends and work didn't mix.

"Aren't you hungry?" she asked, holding her fork in midair.

He tore his gaze away from those puppy-dog eyes and looked at the spread in front of him. "This was very nice of you, Carrie. It looks delicious."

"It tastes great, too, if I say so myself. I helped Gus cook. Kinda miss not having my dad to cook for anymore."

Cash filled his plate and tried not to devour everything in five minutes. He hadn't eaten a meal this good since...since he couldn't remember when. At least with his mouth full he didn't have to talk.

When they'd just about finished, she reached into the basket and pulled out a pumpkin pie and a container of whipped topping.

"Oh, no. I couldn't." He rubbed his full stomach.

"I'm about to burst myself. Maybe we can save it till later." She held the pie in her hand and eyed him shyly. "I edited the employee handbook at home this morning. Just have a few changes to make on the computer and then I can print out a couple drafts. Is it too late for us to work on it today?"

Cash stood and shook his legs, trying to restore some feeling in them. He stared at the blanket again and wished he could curl up on it and take a nap. *Right!* Just what he needed—to get horizontal in his new employee's office. What was wrong with his thinking these days?

"Uh...no. It's not too late. I have plenty to do till you're ready." He bent to help pick up.

"No, that's okay. Just leave it. I'll dispose of the plates and put the leftovers in the fridge. Let's leave the blanket in case we want dessert later." She smiled up at him, but then a curious look came over her face and she busied herself with her task, looking embarrassed again.

"It was very... it was very thoughtful of you to do this, Carrie. Thank you."

She looked up at him briefly as he turned and left. "You're welcome, Cash," she said in a small voice to his back.

Cash. There it was again. But now wasn't the time to tell her to call him Mr. Cunningham, either. He heaved a sigh and returned to his desk.

An hour later Carrie burst into the room and dropped a three-hole-punched bound draft on Cash's desk. Maybe this would make up for her rocky start last week, she thought, watching him scan the contents.

"This looks very thorough," he said, rocking back in his leather chair. "I'll read it right now and we can talk about it Monday."

"I'm going to stick around for a while ... work on some forms that go with it. If you finish and want to discuss it this afternoon, I won't mind staying." How could she wait all weekend for his reaction? Besides, she had nothing better to do. She looked out the window and saw the first hints of rain sprinkled on the glass.

A roll of thunder rumbled across the ocean and Cash eyed her before answering. "Okay, but it'll take me a while to get through all this." He rifled through the thick binder, then looked back to her.

"I have lots to do. Take your time." She darted back to her computer and stared at the flashing cursor.

Why did he make her so nervous? She was doing her best to please him, but so far it hadn't brought the measure of confidence and satisfaction such things usually produced. Instead, she felt anxious, sometimes catching herself holding her breath whenever she was with him. He always made her feel so...so... discombobulated. With her father and Gus, love and acceptance were expected and always there. Maybe that was it. It had been a long time since she'd worked for a stranger.

And strange he was. She started entering data again. One minute he was frowning at her, the next complimenting her. After that T-shirt-and-Christmas-tree episode, she'd thought he might be reconsidering her employment. That was why she'd brought the picnic today—to make amends.

Liar. Her fingers stilled on the keyboard. That wasn't why she'd done it. She'd thought of Cash off and on all day yesterday, wondering whether he was alone for the holiday, what he was doing. She'd already heard the rumors about his parents' boating accident, the one that had left him orphaned as a teenager. She guessed that was why everyone seemed to accept his curt and driven ways.

A lonely pang gripped her heart and Carrie swiveled her chair to the wall. She looked at the photo of herself with her dad, his warm, wrinkled face beaming down at her. Unlike Cash, she at least had a father. She'd been so young when her mother died, it was hard to remember her face, a fact that sometimes left a painful void, but not for long. Dad was more than two parents rolled into one. A tear slid down the side of her face and she wiped it away with the back of her hand. God, how she missed the old guy. Talking with him on the phone yesterday hadn't been the same as feeling his arms around her. She sighed and turned away. He was happy in Maine with his sister and he seemed to be recovering nicely. Those were things to be thankful for... those and all her love-filled memories.

With a wistful smile she pulled herself back to the computer and for the next couple of hours designed one form after another—vacation request, attendance chart, drug screening authorization....

Startled by a pair of legs in her peripheral vision, she stopped and turned. Cash crossed to her desk, the manual in his hands, his jaw muscles working overtime. He looked armed for battle. What had she done now?

"I'm ready to talk if you are." His words were clipped, his eyes dark and furious.

"Of—of course. Here or your office?"

He looked to the corner picnic area, then turned around and marched out, calling over his shoulder, "Mine."

Carrie gathered up her copy, a notepad and pen, and raced around the corner. She sat gingerly in the chair in front of him and waited. What could possibly have caused this sudden change? At lunch he'd seemed almost—

"Turn to the safety section," he barked, and she jumped, her heart somewhere in the vicinity of her larynx.

She flipped the pages, found her place and waited.

"Section 5.7," he said.

She turned to it and read quickly. It was the part about an employee assistance program, providing counseling to those in need—drugs, alcohol, marital, whatever. That must be what had him so bent out of shape—the added cost of the EAP. "Let me explain," she started, feeling relieved it was only money.

"Please do," he snapped.

"Employee assistance programs are standard procedure for most companies that have written drug and alcohol policies. If you notice, in section 5.6—"

"Yes, yes . . . it forbids such behavior on the job or working under the influence . . . and I agree." He folded his arms and let out a long sigh. "But if someone does these things—"

"We get them help," she said, interrupting him. "Evidence proves it's cheaper to provide counseling and possibly rehabilitate a valuable employee than to replace one." She had her statistics down pat. She was ready for this one.

"Maybe so, but not here. *Not* at Cunningham Construction. If someone violates that section, then they're out the door." He stood at that point and started pacing the area in front of the window.

"But, Cash—"

He pivoted in place and glowered at her. "No buts. One violation and they're fired."

He seemed so adamant. Where was this anger coming from? She braved one last argument. "And if it's your best project manager or foreman who's guilty?"

"No exceptions." He strode back to his desk and dropped into the chair. "Besides . . . I know my men better than you do. None of them would do such a thing."

Uh-huh. Now he was clairvoyant. How could someone so successful be so naive?

"I can see by your expression you're not convinced," he said, leaning forward, propping his elbows on the desk and holding her gaze with a dangerous challenge.

She stared back at him, wanting to look away from his angry, dark eyes, but knowing that if she did she'd lose. This was a point she wouldn't cave in on easily. She took her time organizing her thoughts, willing her pulse to return to normal. When it had, with her fingers laced in her lap, she began.

"Let me explain a few things I learned from . . . well, from my dad's attorney." No point in bringing Brian's name into this mess. Cash seemed ready to pounce on her, and she could feel herself growing angry, too. Men! "Can we just talk about it a moment? Without confrontation?"

Cash blinked and his shoulders dropped a notch. With a sigh, he leaned back and crossed an ankle over a knee. "Go ahead. I'm listening."

She let out a long breath of her own and continued. "Over eighty percent of the Fortune 500 companies have some sort of drug and alcohol policy, along with an EAP. While Cunningham Construction is not *that* large, it does employ over two hundred people and it doesn't show any sign of slowing down."

"And this applies to me how?" He was rolling his hand in a fast-forward way that annoyed her.

"If your competitors weed out abusers by preemployment screening and you don't, then you get their rejects when you hire." There! Was *that* to the point?

He seemed to be pondering the new information. His jaw muscles grew still, replaced by a seriously furrowed brow.

"Okay. That makes sense." He leaned forward and cocked his head. "So why not just have preemployment screening, forget the EAP, and fire employees who we suspect of abuse?"

Carrie moved to the edge of her seat and forced herself not to shout. "Because the courts call that wrongful discharge. If you fire someone without testing and documenting evidence, then they sue you and retire to Bora Bora on the damages you'll have to pay."

Cash hiked a corner of his mouth and flashed her a sardonic smile. "You have all the answers, don't you?"

Carrie bit down on her back molars. The man had a problem. And it wasn't her.

When she sat back and didn't reply, he took another tack. "Does the law say I have to have an EAP if I keep these other sections on screening?"

She blew out a sigh of relief. It wasn't the screening he was reacting to. Just as she'd suspected earlier, it was the cost of the EAP that was causing all this hubbub. "No...but if employees fail a drug test—persons you truly want to keep— then you have no place to send them for help when you suspend them. Is that what you want?"

He leaned farther forward with an aggressive posture that made her squirm deeper in her chair. "That's *exactly* what I want."

She swallowed hard, seeing the veins throbbing at his temples and wanting to wrap this up quickly. "Just so I have this right...you want me to keep all the other sections as is, including preemployment screening for applicants and reasonable-suspicion testing of employees? Just cut out the EAP?" She could live with that, but she didn't like it.

He arched an accusatory eyebrow. "What about random screening? I didn't see *that* in here."

She didn't like his tone or the way he pounded at the pages with his rigid index finger. He sounded as though he were begging for a fight, searching for a reason to hang her out to dry for sins she had nothing to do with.

She crossed her arms against her chest and gritted her teeth before speaking. "I purposefully excluded random testing because in the California courts it's just too murky, too regulated. Besides, it's cruel and unusual punishment for longtimers who've never given you a problem." She stood, hoping the conversation was over, not liking the mood he'd put her in.

She started for the door, but he wasn't finished. "I don't know. If applicants have problems, then it would seem logical that some of my employees do, too."

She started tapping her fingers against the door jamb, knowing she was about to lose what little control she had left.

"Why not have one random test when we pass out manuals...catch the guilty parties and clean house?"

She stalked back to his desk and straight-armed both fists against the top of it. "Because it's unfair and illegal and I'll have nothing to do with it." Her voice had been louder than she intended, but it was too late now. He glared up at her from his seat. She could see the idea of firing her dancing across his dark eyes. His breathing was rapid, his jaw working harder than before. She'd challenged him in a way probably no other employee had ever dared to. So be it. Whatever his problem, she wanted no part of it. If it meant finding another job, well . . .

He stood and offered her the manual. "I've made a few notes in the margin on other sections . . . nothing major. If you'll correct those, we'll be done and you can send this thing to the printers."

She snatched the manual from him, turned and left, feeling exhausted. She dropped in her chair and stared at the rain-spattered window.

"Now what on earth was *that* all about?"

The next morning, with the feel of winter nipping at her neck and calves, Carrie bundled her sweater coat around her and quickened her stride. Another block and she'd be back at the pub in time to help Gus restock the bar before opening. The garage had given her the good news she'd hoped for—Woodie would be done late Monday—which meant just one more morning of having Gus schlep her to work.

After all he'd done for her, she planned to do something very special for Gus for Christmas. She turned the key in the handle and yanked hard on the old oak door entrance to M. M. Day's. A gust of warm air and fresh-brewed coffee drew her in with a smile, the soft sounds of Christmas tunes putting her in the mood for making her list and checking it twice. Multicolored lights twinkled from every arch and mirror.

Gus was behind the bar. She crossed to him, giving him a bear hug from behind and eliciting a deep, rolling chuckle.

He turned around and clasped her shoulders. "Ya mean ya not gonna work today?" He chuckled again, then pulled her to him. "I've missed ya, lass."

"Come on." She opened a crate at their feet and pulled out a bottle. "Let me help you stock the bar while we catch up." She reached for a towel on the counter. With a devilish smile, Gus took the clean bottle from her and found a home for it.

"What's that twinkle I see, Gus McGee? Could it have anything to do with last week's dinner with a certain lady?" She turned the side of her face to him and arched an eyebrow, but he ignored her.

He bent down for a bottle of his own to work on. "Why, whatever do ya mean?"

Carrie giggled and slapped the towel at his shoulder. "You're seeing Fran again, aren't you?"

Gus kept working, avoiding her curiosity. "If you want to be helpful, go unlock the door for me. It's time to open." He slapped the keys into her hand and flashed her a quick grin.

She smiled and headed for the door, wondering if she hadn't already found the perfect Christmas present for Gus McGee.

Seven

Monday had gone smoother than any day since she'd started at Cunningham Construction. Cash had been in the office most of the day, and they'd both stayed busy and out of each other's hair. Not a word had been mentioned about Friday's testy encounter. In fact, she'd gotten his stamp of approval on the final draft of the manual without so much as a single comma changed. She'd sent it out for copying and binding, and it would be ready in the morning. Cash even seemed eager for the staff meeting scheduled for three o'clock tomorrow afternoon when the manuals would be distributed.

Best of all, Carrie thought, hooking her arm in Fran's as they bucked a gusty head wind and raced to her car, Woodie was ready and waiting. Fran would drop her off at the garage and then go on to the pub for dinner. Gus had arranged for extra help so he could join them. "Out of courtesy," he'd said, and she'd let him get away with his coyness. By the looks of Fran's high color, Carrie knew her new friend was anticipating a special evening.

When they neared the garage, Carrie asked, "I never heard about your Thanksgiving. Did you enjoy dinner at your niece's?"

Fran wrinkled her nose and kept her eyes on the road. "It was okay. Dinner was nice, but she's got this nerdy-type husband."

Carrie swallowed a chuckle at Fran's choice of words.

"I was really looking forward to watching some football, but he had his mind set on some video he'd rented . . . some foreign thing with subtitles."

Carrie couldn't believe her ears. "You *like* football?"

"Oh, yes. I *love* football. My husband played in college when we first met." She stole a quick peek at Carrie, then turned back to the road. "In truth, I think that's what first attracted me. He looked so handsome in his uniform, those wide, padded shoulders and narrow hips—"

"Why, Fran Wilson . . . I never would have guessed." Carrie giggled, finding it hard to picture this dignified, proper lady all hot and bothered.

"Gus says he gets a big turnout for "Monday Night Football." I've never watched it with a crowd and on a big screen before. Sounds like fun."

Aha! Gus *had* called her since the last time. That sly fox. She knew something was up.

Fran dropped her at the garage and waited for her to come out. A few minutes and hundreds of dollars later, she drove Woodie the short distance to M. M. Day's, parked near Fran and walked to the entrance with her.

Fran looked up and pointed at the sign above the door. "Was that the name of the previous owner?"

Carrie laughed and took Fran's arm as they passed under the bold letters. "No, Gus picked that name. Sort of an advertising gimmick. He thought it would draw in tourists looking for their favorite Carmel resident. Sometimes it actually works. In fact Clint's been here many times."

Fran stopped and faced Carrie. "You mean Clint East-wood?"

Carrie nodded, indicating the array of photos and mem-orabilia on the walls with a sweep of her arm.

Fran gazed around, a frown still creasing her forward. As Gus approached, she whispered to Carrie, "I still don't get the name. What does M. M. Day's have to do with—"

"Well, well. Two of my favorite ladies. Don't that just make my day . . . as my favorite saying goes?"

Fran looked from Gus to Carrie, then back to Gus, a gig-gle bursting from her lips and a rosy glow lighting her high cheekbones. Gus held out his elbow and Fran took it, the pair strolling toward a booth near the screen in the back.

Carrie watched them a moment, her heart warming and aching all at the same time. She turned and headed up the back stairs to change clothes, feeling lonelier than she had since her father had moved east. There had always been someone in her life till lately. Sure, she still had Gus, she tried reassuring herself. She'd been so relieved to be free of Brian, then to find this new home and her new job, to start catching up on her bills, that she'd never given much thought to needing more.

She trudged up the stairs, feeling a pang of envy over Fran's and Gus's new romance. They deserved another shot at love and companionship.

But what about you, S? Brian was out of the question, but that didn't mean she'd given up on men entirely. She let out a sarcastic chuckle. She didn't even *know* an eligible bachelor. She opened the door to her apartment and dropped onto the sofa, knowing she'd just told herself an-other lie, which she seemed to be doing a lot of lately. With her elbows on her knees she covered her face with her hands, but the vision lingered. He sat cross-legged on the blanket, eating leftover turkey, his blue eyes shining. . . .

Suddenly she jumped up as though shot from a cannon. She changed quickly into boots and jeans, looked at the Cunningham T-shirt, then tossed it aside in favor of an old

49ers jersey, which she pulled over her head as she raced back out the door and down the steps. Enough of this fiddle-faddle. Who needs a man, anyway?

Carrie stood on the side of the road and kicked Woodie's front tire.

"After all I've done for you!" She kicked again, then turned her back to the passenger door, leaned against it and crossed her arms. "Why didn't you tell me they'd run your gas tank down to nothing?" She was sure it had been over half-full when she left it at the garage. She watched a steady stream of cars pass on the opposite side of Woodie, no one slowing or looking her way.

Another ten minutes passed and no one stopped to help her. There wasn't a gas station for at least a couple of miles. She bunched her fists at the open neck of her trench coat, pulling the thin fabric closer to her and dancing from one foot to the other in an attempt to keep warm. Then she spotted the cream-colored van with the familiar cypress logo pulling off the side of the road, and she waved her arms wildly over her head.

"Sam! Am I glad to see you." The shop foreman sauntered toward her, seemingly in no hurry. "Do you happen to have a can of gas in your van?"

"Sure. Let me get it." He shot her a look of disdain, then walked back to the van slower than before, his steps almost measured, too precise.

As she watched him pour gas into Woodie, she thought about asking him if he'd been out to a site already or if he was late, too. If memory served her, he'd been late to work often in her short tenure. Yet, under the circumstances, it didn't seem the time or place for such a question. So when he finished, she simply thanked him and drove off, watching him in her rearview mirror as he took his sweet time getting back into his van.

Of all days to be late, she groaned, pulling to an abrupt stop in the parking lot ten minutes later. She'd meant to discuss today's activities with Cash before she left last night, but she'd forgotten all about it. Apparently he hadn't read her first newsletter yet, or surely he would have said something. According to Fran, who had worked at Cunningham since day one, today's events would be a first.

Carrie laughed as she ran the short distance from Woodie to the front door. It would be a first for her, too. But, heck, it sounded like fun, it didn't cost anything and it was bound to keep morale up. Things had turned out so well at the tree-trimming, there was no reason to think Bring Your Pet to Work Day couldn't be just as successful.

She waited for the elevator, recounting the rules. Pets must be in cages or on short leashes and kept in the owner's area. If they got loud or disruptive they'd have to be taken home.

She'd made three separate boxes—one each for dogs, cats and other—then drew one name from each. Obviously everyone couldn't do this on the same day. That was why the newsletter said a few would get their chance on the first Tuesday of each month.

Today, December 1, would be the trial run. The elevator opened and Carrie rode to the third floor. She smiled, imagining how things would go. Employees who never spoke to each other would act like old friends after stopping by to see the other's pet. She'd seen it work on the street often enough. Strangers wouldn't talk to strangers, but they'd stop to pet a dog and eventually strike up a friendly conversation. Cash might be a little taken aback, but he'd see. It would work out just—

The door slid open and Carrie saw Peggy crying hysterically at her desk. Carrie ran behind the desk and threw her arms around the young woman's heaving shoulders. "Peggy! What's happened?"

Peggy pointed to the empty bird cage behind her. Between sobs and hiccups she said, "Tweety... He was...sitting on...my finger." She buried her face in Carrie's coat lapels. "He flew off when he . . . when he heard Jane's cat yowl."

Carrie patted Peggy on the back, then sat her down at her desk. "Blow your nose, Peggy, and wipe your eyes. You just stay put and cover the phones. I'll find Tweety. Okay?"

Peggy opened a bottom drawer and grabbed a handful of tissues. "B-but . . . there's a cat in accounting." She started to sob again. "And—and a boa constrictor in the shop."

An ugly image of a big lump in the snake's throat made Carrie's stomach turn, but she put up a good front. "But neither of them can fly. I bet Tweety's found a nice high safe spot. Don't you worry. I'll go find him and be right back." As an afterthought she turned back and grabbed the cage, wondering how she'd coax the little guy inside it.

She ran past Cash's open office door, grateful he was no-where in sight. Shrugging out of her coat, she tossed it on the chair, then headed toward the end of the hall leading to accounting. If Jane's cat was contained then one disaster could be eliminated.

When she entered Jane's area, she blew out a sigh of re-lief. Fred was cuddled in a ball on Jane's lap as she worked away at her accounts. His harness was firmly in place, a connecting leash tethered to a desk leg. Jane looked from the cage in Carrie's hand to her face.

"Oh-oh. Problem?" Jane asked.

"One missing Tweety. Keep a reign on Fred and page me if you hear any wings flapping." Carrie ran on toward the shop, praying Hoser the boa hadn't found any treats to feast on.

She walked as fast as her legs would carry her, heeding the No Running signs posted in the shop, till she spotted the back of Jack's head bent over his bench. She braced herself for the worst while looking around for Hoser. She stopped behind Jack, her heart in her throat.

"Where is he?" she asked, catching her breath.

"Carrie! I was hoping you'd stop by." He stepped away from his bench and pointed underneath. "Ain't he somethin'?"

Carrie stared at the endless fat body in the large wire cage. She let out a long breath along with a shiver. "He sure is." Snakes had never been her idea of a household pet, but to each his own. She looked up at Jack's beaming smile. "Has he been like this all morning?" she asked.

"Yep. Hasn't moved an inch."

Carrie patted him on the shoulder. "If you see a stray parakeet, have me paged, will you?"

Jack looked at the empty bird cage and nodded. "Sure will, Carrie. See ya later."

She waved over her head with her free hand and retraced her steps. Maybe Tweety had found his way back to Peggy, or someone else had found him and cornered him in a closed room or closet. That was probably what had happened, she convinced herself as she passed her office on the way to Peggy's.

She noticed the shut door to Cash's office, which meant he'd arrived. Thank God he always used the back stairs, or he would have seen Peggy's puffy eyes, or worse yet, been met by her wailing. At the moment all seemed quiet. She had a good feeling about this. She tiptoed by, relieved he couldn't see the empty cage in her hand. It would be much easier if the problem was resolved before he learned about Bring Your Pet to Work Day.

Before rounding the corner, Carrie closed her eyes and pictured Tweety perched on Peggy's finger, as if willing it to be true. She made the turn and saw Peggy staring at the phone, her face composed, but no sign of Tweety. Peggy eyed Carrie with a look that spoke volumes. It wasn't grief in Peggy's eyes. It was—

"Is she back yet?" Cash's angry voice came over the intercom on Peggy's phone.

"Y-yes, sir. She just got here." Peggy avoided Carrie's eyes, twirling a loose strand of blond hair around her finger.

"Tell her to get in here right now...with that cage. And tell her to shut the door behind her."

"Y-yes, sir."

Without comment Carrie did an about-face and raced back to his office, shutting the door quickly. With the bird cage peeking out from behind her legs her gaze flitted around the room, searching for the cause of all this hubbub. She braved a quick glance at Cash, and he motioned with his head to the top shelf alongside his desk. If ever there were a man about to explode, it was this one. His nostrils were flaring and his eyes had her pinned to the wall, rendering her speechless and immobile.

Something had to be done—and done quickly. And she knew who had to do it. "M-may I borrow your chair a moment?" He didn't move. "I think if I stand on it with the cage right in front of the shelf I can get Tweety back inside."

He stood reluctantly and stepped aside. "Be my guest."

Carrie removed her plum-colored pumps and hiked her matching skirt above her knees far enough to make the awkward climb. The chair started to roll backward, and Cash was quick to brace his legs against the front of it and hold the arms firmly in place. Slowly she straightened and brought the cage up above her head. The frightened parakeet retreated to the back of the shelf, making a small, terrified peep.

"Come on Tweety. I won't hurt you," she coaxed. "Mama's waiting in the next room, and she'll give you a special treat if you'll be a good boy." Carrie angled her body farther toward the shelf, and her slick, hose-covered feet slipped backward.

Instinctively Cash threw his arms around her legs and held them tight. "Hurry up before you break your neck," he snapped.

"Okay, okay. Hand me a ruler."

He released one hand long enough to follow her instruction, then resumed his firm grip.

On tiptoe, Carrie pressed the cage to the front of the shelf with one hand and, using the ruler, carefully nudged Tweety forward. Quickly she slammed the cage door shut, Tweety safely inside, then released a long sigh.

It wasn't till then that she felt Cash's warm hands above her knees, those long, graceful fingers holding her tight. Before she could move, his hands slid over her skirt to her waist and he lowered her to the floor. Her backside slid down the front of him in one fluid second, the movement leaving her legs shaking in the narrow space between him and the chair. Her breath hitched in her throat as the first of several hiccups escaped her lips.

If only she could walk out of here backward, never meeting his eyes. Her cheeks burned and tears threatened behind her closed lids. Last week she knew he'd debated firing her. She'd been hanging on by a narrow thread ever since. Now this. Yet at this moment, standing so close to him, her job was playing second fiddle to the taut strum of her heartbeat.

Slowly she turned, forcing the bird cage between them, hoping, praying, he couldn't see her face. "I—I'm sorry about this, Cash. It never should have happened. I take full responsibility." He was going to fire her. She knew it.

Cash took her by the elbow and escorted her around his desk, depositing her in a side chair. When he sat in his own chair, she braved a glance. Gone was the tension she'd seen in his face earlier, which only confused her further. She sat very quietly, staring at Tweety, wishing she could crawl in beside the frightened little bird.

After what seemed an eternity, Cash started chuckling.

Chuckling! She couldn't believe her ears. When she finally looked up, he was pointing to a spot in the center of a blueprint spread across his desk. Tweety's signature was splattered across it.

"Cash, I'm so sorry... about this whole mess." She lowered her gaze, then peeked up at him. "I guess this wasn't one of my better ideas."

His smile widened. "On that we agree."

He wasn't ranting and raving. He wasn't throwing her out on her ear. Who was this man who masqueraded as Cash Cunningham? The old one had wreaked enough havoc with her overactive fantasies, but this one...

"Go give...Tweety...back to Peggy and ask her to take him home. Tell her to take an early lunch and then get back here. Okay?" He lowered his head and peered up at her from beneath his thick, dark brows. It was a look of empathy, not rage, which left her numb and confused. With great effort she pulled herself up and out of the chair, Tweety now fluttering about wildly, voicing a steady protest.

"When you're done with that, come back in and we'll talk."

Ah, now she understood. The calm before the storm.

Oh, S, what have you done now?

Eight

Carrie leaned forward in Cash's side chair, her hands tucked beneath her thighs, staring at the floor. There was no denying she'd screwed up.

"First, I'll need another page of this blueprint. You'll have to drive over to Salinas and try to talk them out of a new page 17. They may make you buy the whole set, so take a check with you, just in case."

"Cash, I'm really —"

He held a hand up and stopped her. "But before you leave, round up the rest of the pets and ask their owners to take them home. Now." She looked up sheepishly. "No more pets at work. Agreed?"

She nodded slowly, waiting for him to lower the boom. But instead, he slapped his desk and laughed so loud that she couldn't hold back her own laughter, which was more from embarrassment than amusement.

Finally Cash rubbed his eyes with the backs of his hands

and smiled at her. Smiled! The iceman, the everything-in-its-place man. Laughing and smiling. Go figure.

"Look, I can't say I approve of what you did today, but it took a lot of imagination, that's for sure." He laughed again, then regained control. "After the success of last Wednesday's tree-trimming and those T-shirts...which, by the way, I'm still hearing rave reviews about...well—" he rocked back in his chair "—I think you might be on to something."

She felt a ton of concrete lift from her shoulders and chest.

"I showed the manual to my attorney this weekend and he said it was a work of art. He wanted to know what law school you went to. Actually, the words he used were 'It's a masterpiece.' He accused me of having another attorney draft it."

Carrie started playing with her fingernails, thinking of the hours she'd spent with Brian, going over her dad's manual with a fine-tooth comb. But for some reason she had no desire to tell Cash about Brian.

"In the short time you've been here, you've accomplished more than I ever expected. This morning wasn't your best move, but we all make mistakes."

Who had possessed this man's body? This couldn't possibly be the same person. Could it?

"From now on, why don't you show me the newsletter before you copy and distribute it. If there's a problem, it will be easier to discuss it then. Now—" he shifted in his chair, acting as though the incident were over and it were no big thing "—I have something else I'd like to discuss."

So did she. Like Sam, and a few others she'd observed. On the drive in she'd decided she should share her suspicions, but now didn't seem the time. Instead, she held Cash's steady gaze, noticing again how very blue his eyes were. She liked his square jaw, too, and the few strands of dark hair that sometimes fell carelessly across his forehead. Like now.

"There's a seminar next week in San Francisco...runs from Wednesday through Friday." He turned his chair sideways and looked out the glass wall. "It deals with a myriad of personnel matters, including the implementation of drug and alcohol policies and employee assistance programs. I thought you might like to go."

She slid forward in her chair. "I'd love to!"

"I thought you would, so I made reservations. It will be held at the St. Francis. I had Peggy send in our registrations and reserve a couple rooms."

Carrie sat stunned, not knowing what to say as a sudden tingling streaked down her spine. After a moment she said, "I love the St. Francis. It's such a grand old place." Her voice sounded weak and unenthused to her own ears. She hoped it didn't sound that way to Cash. This was exciting news, it was just that...

He spun back to his desk, his eyes cast down. "Well, if we're done here, I have work to do and you have to get to Salinas." He picked up a pen, and her gaze riveted on his long, gentle fingers. "While you're gone I'll finish making notes for this afternoon's staff meeting." Without looking up, he added, "By the way, the manuals arrived earlier and are in the conference room. They look sensational."

Carrie rose and headed for the door. "Th-thank you, Cash."

"You're welcome, Carrie. See you at the meeting," he said to her back.

Bad idea, Cash thought, watching Carrie's trim figure clear his doorway. He remembered her shapely thighs inches from his face, and the way his hands had fit around her small waist, riding the curves of her hips as he lifted her off his chair and onto the floor.

Now he'd told her they'd be spending a couple of days alone...in a romantic hotel...out of town.

He turned back to the glass and stared at the breaking waves far below. He didn't know which bothered him more—the fact that he was putting himself in a tempting situation, or the fact that he'd always forbidden intercompany dating—a policy Carrie had incorporated in the manual that he was about to distribute this very day. He had no one to blame but himself for leaving that one in. She'd merely picked it up from one of his old memos.

Thinking back, it had seemed like a good idea at the time. Enough men had hit on previous secretaries, and vice versa, to justify it. He swiveled away from the view, recalling one ambitious receptionist who had set her sights on him. Her skills were exceptional. If only she'd limited them to office work.

He pulled himself higher in his chair. Yep. That policy was still a good idea. Now, with all the sexual harassment cases, he'd be opening Pandora's box to allow dating among employees.

He thought about Carrie again and started doodling her name next to his meeting notes. Then he slapped the pen down.

No. There could be no exceptions. Talk about company gossip! He'd ruin whatever respect he had left. Besides, if it didn't work out with her, he'd risk losing one of the brightest and hardest-working employees he'd ever hired if she decided to quit. His gaze fixed on one of her handwritten memos and the debate in his head raged on.

When was the last time he'd even considered dating someone? He couldn't remember. In his twenties, that was all he could think about whenever he wasn't working. Now there never seemed time. And recalling his mother and her free-spending friends, he wasn't sure there was trust, either. One of his father's pearls of wisdom sprang to the forefront: *Remember, son, women are the ruination of all good men!*

Restless, Cash pushed out of his chair and started pacing in front of the glass. He certainly didn't have his father's poor work ethics, or much of anything else he'd possessed, either. Still, it had been a long time since anyone had seen

Cash Cunningham at a singles' bar. And when he worked
out at the gym, he stuck to the men's area, concentrating on
his reason for being there and nothing else.

He stopped in front of his chair, then dropped with a
weary sigh. All work and no play. *Cunningham, you* have
become a dull boy.

With all the willpower he could muster, he applied himself to the task in front of him, using business to fill the
vacuum that surrounded his heart.

As usual.

When Peggy's voice came over the intercom, reminding
him it was a quarter to three, he looked at his watch in disbelief. His notepad lay beside a pile of correspondence ready
to be typed and mailed. Not only was he ready for the
meeting, he'd polished off the entire contents of his in-
basket. His stomach growled, and he opened his bottom
drawer for the jar of peanuts he always kept there. He
poured a small handful, then popped them into his mouth.
Crunching quickly, he scanned his notes, then picked up the
pad and headed for the conference room.

The few employees still at their desks scurried out of their
chairs and followed Cash. When he entered the room, a
hush fell over it, and he felt all eyes focus on him as he
dropped his notepad on the podium. He looked up and saw
latecomers standing around the perimeter of the packed
room. To his far right, Carrie and Peg stood behind a long
table, the manuals stacked neatly in manageable piles in
front of them.

"Good afternoon," he said, feeling suddenly stodgy and
stiff.

The room responded just as formally. "Good afternoon," everyone said in unison, making him feel like a
teacher in front of a class. He shifted his weight behind the
podium, gripping the top with his fingers.

He looked back at his notes, thumbing through the
countless pages. Hearing the shuffle of feet under chairs and

impatient sighs, he tossed his notes on the table beside him and picked up a manual.

"I had planned to go over this with you, but rather than put you to sleep I think I'll let you read it on your own." He looked around the room and saw relief on many faces. "Most of what's in here you have received over the years in various memos, so there will be few surprises." He placed the manual on the podium and stepped from behind it. "There is one new section, though, that I feel needs some explanation."

At this Cash watched his employees straighten in their chairs, a mixture of curiosity and concern on different faces. Slowly, cautiously, he explained the preemployment drug screening, noticing many relax as they learned it didn't apply to them.

When he got to the part about testing existing employees for drugs and alcohol under certain conditions, he could feel the mood shift. There was a tension in the room that was nearly palpable. As clearly and quickly as he could, he explained there wouldn't be random testing, only testing when there was a reasonable suspicion that someone had violated the policy. This seemed to satisfy some, but still he felt the tension in the room. He fell silent for a moment, weighing the wisdom of his next words. They weren't on his notepad. He hadn't planned to make this offer. But suddenly he knew he had to, in spite of a feeling of impending disaster. He walked behind the podium and gripped the sides for support.

"These policies have been added for the safety and well-being of all our employees. While I feel certain most of you have never abused substances and this section will never affect you—" He paused and looked at Carrie, but she only stared at the pile of manuals in front of her. He had the sinking feeling she'd been right—he'd buried his head in the sand about this issue. But not any longer. "If anyone is battling a problem...even here at the workplace—" Whatever shuffling had been going on stopped. Dead silence and lowered gazes filled the room. "I'm inviting you to stop by my office over the next few days. Anyone who's honest enough to confide in me will earn my highest respect...and I'll do my best to see that you get whatever help you need to deal with your problem and keep your job."

Having said the most difficult part—a part he'd never planned nor believed he could say—he stepped from behind the podium again and took in the room.

"But let me add this. If you don't come forward now and you get caught later, there will be no second chance." He let his gaze move slowly from face to face, making eye contact with as many as braved a look.

The silence was long and threatening. He hadn't anticipated this, and now he didn't know how to conclude. If he dismissed them now, there could be a pile of resignations on his desk in the morning.

In his peripheral vision he caught movement. Then there was a slight tap on his arm. He looked down at Carrie as she spoke softly at his side.

"Can I say something?"

He wanted to kiss her on the cheek and say *Please do.* Instead, he laid a hand on her shoulder and turned back to the solemn faces. "I'm sure by now you've all met Carrie Sargent, our new Human Resources Manager." Many smiles appeared, and Cash pushed on. "Carrie has written other manuals such as this one and would like to add a few words." Relieved, he stepped aside and let Carrie have center stage.

"It's not unusual to feel a little apprehensive about what you've just heard. Let me explain our motivation."

Cash watched her gaze flick across the room, and the body language of the people in front of her relaxed. It was amazing. They hardly knew this woman, but it was obvious they liked and trusted her as though she'd been here all her life.

"I'll cut right to the heart of the matter. Many of you deal with heavy and potentially dangerous equipment. None of us would want to be near an operator under the influence, would we?'' She shook her head and many followed suit, some calling out, "No way..." "Not me..."

"I don't blame you. Neither would I. So for safety reasons we must be absolutely certain no one shows up for work who's not fully capable of performing their job."

She paused a moment and glanced back to Cash, looking for all the world as though she'd prefer talking with him first before adding her next words. Instinctively he nodded for her to proceed. Then, in the space of a heartbeat, he wondered when that trust and these other feelings he was having had begun.

"A moment ago Cash made the offer to come talk with him if you have a problem. Let me expand on that offer. If you have *any* concerns or questions about anything you read in here—" she held up a manual "—then we want you to stop by for that, too. The door is open to all of you—for any reason. Okay?'' That prompted several nods and a few verbal okays.

"Good. Now, when we're finished, form lines in front of the stacks and we'll give each of you a manual and have you sign and date a form that says you received it." She turned to Cash. "Is there anything else?"

Cash caught himself smiling at Carrie as she turned to him. A feeling of pride ran through him. It hadn't been a mistake to hire this spunky woman. In fact...

Remembering her question, he regrouped quickly, having already decided to end on a lighter note.

"Just this." He forced his smile to stay in place as he looked back to his restless workers. "It was quite a surprise to see that tree in the atrium last Wednesday." There were a few titters from the back of the room. "I want to thank all of you for bringing decorations from home. The entrance never looked more beautiful." He saw some jaws drop in disbelief. "And one last thing... don't forget to wear your T-shirts this Friday. Thanks for your attention.... Now you can get your books."

Cash made a hasty exit, but all the way down the hall he heard applause mixed with enthusiastic chatter.

There it was again. That lump in his throat. He was getting soft in his old age. When he reached his office, he shut the door behind him and walked to the glass. Below, a strong wind had branches bent to the extreme, making trees look as though they were running from the sea. He couldn't blame them. It was a force to be reckoned with. As was this business lately.

Things used to seem black-and-white within these four walls. Now he saw many grays. Before today he would have bet his bottom dollar there wasn't an employee at Cunningham Construction who would dare use drugs or alcohol before or during work. From the tension in the room he'd just left, he was no longer certain. He could feel the fear, as if everyone had thought he was talking about him or her when he suggested a few might have problems. Was he imagining what he'd seen looking into their faces? Worse yet, what if he was right?

It didn't take twenty-four hours for the parade to start. There was a steady stream of employees coming and going through Cash's door with a frequency that made all other work impossible. Peggy started a waiting list and began calling people when they were nearing their turn.

At eleven Friday morning Cash buzzed Peg on the intercom. "Tell the next one to make it two o'clock. Then schedule everyone at fifteen-minute intervals till we get to the end."

"Okay, boss."

"And hold my calls till then, too."

"Will do."

Cash stood and arched his back, looking at the tubes full of blueprints standing next to his desk. He might miss a few bids because of all this, but at the moment, nothing else was more important. He walked to the wall adjacent to Carrie's office and listened. When he heard movement, he decided it was time for a talk.

He strode in and shut the door behind him, dropping wearily into the chair in front of her desk. Carrie stilled her fingers on the keyboard and eyed him cautiously.

"I'm in trouble, aren't I?"

"Why would you say that?"

"I've seen all the traffic at your door. You can't be getting anything else done." He watched her tuck curls behind her ears and avoid his eyes.

"Carrie." He stopped and waited for her to meet his gaze. When she did, he saw a glaze over the most beautiful green eyes he'd ever seen. She pulled a tissue from a drawer and blew her nose.

"You're not in trouble," he said, surprised at her reaction.

She sniffed. "Things were so much quieter around here before—"

"Before I took my head out of the sand. It's not very easy to see or hear in that position." She dabbed at her eyes and rewarded him with a small smile. "In fact, I'm the one who messed up." Had he ever said that before? Never to an employee, that he could remember. "Anyway, we've got to talk about the EAP."

She looked at him confused. "Cash . . . we have no EAP. You asked me to cut it out, remember?"

He slouched in the chair. "Exactly. That's where I messed up. I'm not equipped to counsel these people." He gestured toward the wall behind him as if they were still lined up outside.

"There are so many problems that seem to be interfering with performance. Some say they're late because of this, or staring at the ceiling half the day because of that. And . . . well, a few say they know of someone abusing substances . . . either just before work or even during. I'm not sure if they mean themselves or someone else. They're afraid to say. Instead they've been asking what will happen to these

people.... How will I help them? Will they keep their jobs?"
He rose from the chair and started pacing.

After a few more silent turns, Carrie said, "It's never too
late to add an employee assistance plan."

He stopped and crossed his arms on the top of her computer. "How fast can we get one? Where do we find providers? How much will it cost? And how—"

"Slow down, cowboy." She looked as if she were struggling to contain a laugh. At least she had the grace not to
say, "I told you so."

She stood and started rummaging through a file cabinet
beside her desk. "I have brochures from several providers,
and I called a few for quotes. Let me see . . ."

Cash glanced at his watch. "I'm in the mood for some of
Day's clam chowder. Are you?"

Carrie looked up from the folder in her hand. "Now?
Can we spare the time?"

"My next appointment isn't till two. Grab your folder and
we'll discuss it on the way down to Carmel and over lunch."
She was staring at him, dumbstruck. "Unless you already
made plans for—"

"No. No, I don't have other plans." She tucked the folder
under her arm and shut the cabinet drawer with her hip.
"Let's go."

Nine

———

Carrie peeked at him from the passenger seat of his Mercedes. Was this a Cash clone or the real thing? In the past week she'd witnessed kindness and sensitivity from this man—not just when dealing with her, but with everyone. Not once had he complained about the steady flow of employees visiting his office with their problems, keeping him away from his work.

She stole another look, this time longer. She loved his clean-cut all-American look. She could almost picture him using a hand razor on that close-shaven square jaw. Nothing electric about this man. Unless she counted his blue eyes. He glanced at her, then turned his face back to the highway.

"Something wrong?" he asked.

"Oh! N-no. Not a thing. Just enjoying the scenery." Well, it was true. Except the best scenery was behind the wheel. *Not smart, S.* This line of thinking had to stop. This second.

"Want a short recap of my favorite EAP providers?" she asked.

"It's that, or go back to school for my degree in psychiatry." His expression took on a worried look. "I never would have dreamed so many of my people had such serious problems—divorce, depression, troubled teens. I know there's some of that everywhere, but this substance-abuse thing has me most concerned."

They drove south for a distance, the weight of the problems permeating the small space around them, a heavy silence thickening the air. After a while Carrie briefed him on the services and costs of a few EAPs.

Cash found a parking spot near the pub, and opened the door for Carrie before she could gather her material and step out. "So you mean they're not just for drug or alcohol problems?"

Carrie slid out, the folder protruding from her briefcase-style purse. "Oh, heavens no. They cover all those other issues you mentioned, too."

Their eyes held briefly and she thought his mind was no longer on EAPs. When she realized neither was hers, she walked into Day's ahead of him and waved to Gus who was drying glasses behind the bar. His eyebrows shot up before he waved back, and she could see the devil in his expression even from a distance.

"Remember that first time you were here?" she whispered to Cash as they slid into an empty booth.

"How could I forget?" His laugh was low and easy. And it sounded a tad more intimate than she remembered before, which did nothing to calm Carrie's nerves. This suddenly felt more like a date than a business lunch.

Gus came over, drying his hands on a white towel and smiling from ear to ear, which didn't help a bit. "You two havin' lunch today?"

"No, we thought we'd just drive down and spy on you...see if you were flirting with some lady at the bar." Carrie winked at him and laughed. "We'd both like big bowls of Carmel's greatest clam chowder, and I'll have a diet Coke.''

"Make that two," Cash said.

"I think I can keep that straight. But about that flirtin' stuff, lass," Gus said, ruffling the top of Carrie's hair, "well, ya know Frannie wouldn't like that. I'm a one-woman kinda man." He winked as he turned away.

Carrie eyed Cash, then quickly lowered her gaze.

"Was there something I missed?" he asked after an awkward moment.

"Just the 'Frannie' part." She didn't think it was a secret. Still, she felt a little as if she were telling stories out of school.

"Do I know this Frannie person?" He was smiling at her in a mischievous way. Was he flirting or was it her overactive imagination?

Gus reappeared with their Cokes and silverware and she breathed a sigh of relief.

"Chowder will be right up." He started to leave, then leaned in toward Carrie's ear. "If ya see Frannie when ya get back, ask her if she'll call me on her break. I got an idea for tomorrow night." He walked off, leaving Carrie staring at Cash. She could feel the color creeping up her neck.

Cash lowered his chin and squinted at her. "No! Really?"

"Really."

He shook his head and started to laugh. "Well, I'll be damned." He slapped the table, then lifted his Coke and downed half of it. "What a week of surprises. Tell me . . . is there anything else I should know about my employees?"

She could feel her own smile slip away when she thought of Sam. She hadn't shared her suspicions, and she wasn't sure this was the right time. She wasn't even sure she was right.

Gus placed steaming bowls in front of each of them. "Enjoy."

"Carrie?" Cash looked at her out of the corner of his eye. "I can see those wheels turning. What aren't you telling me?"

She blew on a spoonful of chowder and debated how much to tell him. She was just about ready to answer when she cast a look up the aisle and spotted a familiar figure. She dropped her spoon into the soup and turned to the wall, fidgeting with the folder in her purse, hiding her face as best she could.

But it was too late. He didn't pass.

He slid in beside her and thrust a possessive arm around her shoulder. "Carrie! I can't believe I caught you."

Carrie shrugged out from under his arm and shot him her best drop-dead look, but it didn't work. He kissed her on the cheek before turning to Cash and thrusting out his arm.

"Name's Brian Underwood. And yours?"

Carrie watched helplessly as her ex-fiancé turned on the charm, knowing full well the impression he hoped to convey to this male competitor.

"Cash . . . Cash Cunningham," he said evenly, sizing up the intruder.

Brian laughed. "No kidding?"

Carrie watched Cash grind his teeth before he responded. "Uh . . . Brian . . . this is a working lunch. . . ."

"Ahhh . . . So that's it." He looked at Carrie. "Your new boss? Why didn't you tell me, sweetheart?" He turned back to Cash. "My fiancée is full of surprises."

"Brian! You're not—"

"—going to intrude on your job one more second." He gave her another quick peck on the cheek and stood abruptly. "Talk to you later. And Cash—" he leaned on the unusual name and laughed sardonically "—nice meeting you." He strode off without a backward glance.

"Cash . . . let me explain," she started.

He shook his head and picked up his spoon. "No need. I would expect a young—" he looked away, then back

"—woman like yourself to have a private life. You don't owe me any explanation."

He ate his soup, one spoonful after the other. No small talk. Not even a casual glance in her direction.

Gus dropped off the check and Cash paid, sliding from the booth the second he had. He stepped back and waited for her to precede him, which she did, her stomach having difficulty in processing the chowder.

What did it matter that Brian was her *ex*-fiancé? Why did she care that Cash didn't know it was over? More puzzling, why had *his* mood changed so abruptly? Had she been right earlier when she thought he was flirting with her? If she had, then Brian's announcement—erroneous as it was—made him think she was taken!

She shook her head and kept walking. Men!

She didn't wait for Cash to open the door. She stalked out of Day's and stood at the car door till he pointed his key chain and it yipped at the lock. She let herself in and folded her arms across her chest, wishing they were back at work and not confined to this small space in such close proximity.

Cash pulled away from the curb and didn't back off the gas till they were halfway to Monterey. Finally he let out a long breath, then said, "You were about to tell me something before—" he shot her a quick glance "—just after Gus brought our soup. What was it?"

Sam. Drat! She'd forgotten all about that. She wished Cash had, too. Now, with him in his current mood, it was definitely the wrong time to share her suspicions. Her mind raced for a neutral answer. When one came, she started hesitantly.

"In…uh…one seminar I learned that…uh…well, they said that repeated absenteeism and lateness, especially on Mondays, was sometimes a symptom of a substance problem." She didn't have to say Sam's name. Maybe Cash would figure it out for himself.

"Yes. I remember those things on your sample list of reasonable suspicion—justification for a drug test. So who are we talking about here?"

Right for the jugular. Now this was the Cash she'd first met. Must be a Gemini—two distinct personalities, completely opposite...

"Well? Are you going to tell me or keep me guessing?"

She exhaled loud enough that he had to know he'd won. "Last Tuesday...when I was late because—"

"Yes, yes. Get to the point."

The point is...you're acting like a jerk. "Sam saw me on the side of the road and stopped to put gas in my tank."

Cash glanced over, his eyes narrow slits. Then he looked back to the road. She saw his jaw muscles flexing, but he said nothing.

"He walked very slowly back to his van...the way people walk when they're having difficulty navigating and don't want anyone to notice. And I'm fairly certain I smelled alcohol on his breath." There. Right or wrong, she'd told him. She watched the side of his face and could almost hear his train of thought as he tried to remember how many days Sam had been late or hadn't shown up at all...

Cash parked and got out of the car, and she raced to keep up with him. He took the back stairs two at a time, then paused at her door only briefly, his eyes riveted on his watch. "It's five to and I have appointments all afternoon. We'll talk more Monday." He entered his office and shut the door with a thud.

What a first-class jerk! Cash paced from one end of his office to the other, trying to decide whether he was referring to himself or Brian Underwood. Underwood. Humph. That was exactly where he'd like to put the guy—under a couple of cords of dark and dirty wood. He stopped pacing, his jaw slack at the very notion of having imagined such an unfathomable act. So what if she was engaged? He should be relieved.

Yet relief wasn't the emotion he was feeling.

"Employees are off-limits, dummy," he said aloud. When was he going to lock away these fantasies and forget them? He walked to the glass wall and stared sightlessly at the ocean, remembering his other problem.

Sam. Please, not Sam. He was the first foreman hired. He'd been with Cunningham Construction from day one. She had to be wrong.

But in his heart he knew she wasn't.

The more he thought about it on the drive home that night, the more he remembered. Not only had there been increased absences, but he thought he'd smelled liquor on Sam's breath at the tree-trimming. At the time he'd dismissed it, sure he was wrong. But throughout the weekend more examples leaped from Cash's memory bank, each pointing in the same direction.

Monday morning Cash stopped for breakfast and pushed scrambled eggs around his plate, but mostly he stared into his black coffee. He hadn't been late a single morning since he started the company. Today was different. Dread weighed on his back and shoulders, as heavy as any anchor, rooting him to his seat longer than he'd planned. Sam wasn't just any employee. He'd helped build Cunningham Construction into the success it was today. Somewhere along the way he'd become a surrogate father, encouraging, guiding, supporting—things his own dad never had the time or the sobriety to offer.

Now Sam. There was this vague sense of abandonment, and along with it the memory of the last bottle Cash had seen lifted to his father's lips, just before . . .

He paid the tab and walked to his car. A heavy fog rolled in from the sea, matching his mood, keeping alive memories best forgotten.

It was nearly ten o'clock by the time Cash ran up the back steps and walked directly to Peg's desk, breezing past Carrie's and his own office.

"Morning, Peg."

"Morning, Mr. Cunningham."

"Find Sam for me, will you? Have him come to my office right away."

Cash strode to his office, eager to occupy his area of sovereignty. Once inside, he hung his trench coat on the hanger behind the door and sat down. Somehow, in here, within these four walls, he'd sort it all out and do the right thing. He was no sooner settled than a small knock came from the other side of the door.

"Mr. Cunningham? May I come in?"

He heard the air rush out of his lungs and passed his lips. "Sure, Peg."

She stepped just inside the doorway, her hand still on the knob. "I talked to the shop...." Her hand was trembling, and so was her voice.

"Peg...what is it?" He stood and walked around his desk, knowing that whatever it was, it wasn't good.

"Jack said you should get down there right away. Sam cut his arm and he's screaming like a lunatic at Carrie—"

He didn't need to hear more. He ran to the stairs, down the three flights and along the wide corridor leading to the shop. Shouts could be heard through the closed swinging doors ahead. Anxiety crowded the back of his throat, leaving his mouth dry. His breath came in jagged currents as he raced the last few yards. This wasn't going to be pretty. In his gut he already knew what would happen today. Yet all the hours of thinking, rationalizing and planning hadn't helped him one iota. He still wasn't prepared to deal with Sam. With both hands he pushed beyond the swinging doors and then froze.

Blood oozed from Sam's left arm. Carrie trembled in front of him, her face devoid of color, her white silk blouse spattered with blood. She was staring, wide-eyed, at the broken bottle in Sam's shaking right hand.

Ten

Carrie's gaze darted to Cash in the doorway, her head not moving. He was walking as though in slow motion. Was she hallucinating or was he truly here? He walked closer and she saw his eyes. They were no longer vivid blue, but darker than midnight. Still he didn't look at her. He was looking at Sam, his stare high above the jagged bottle, almost as if he hadn't seen it. Surely he had, she prayed.

"Sam," Cash said calmly. "Looks like you had a little accident here." He walked closer, his focus now on the foreman's cut arm.

"Yeah. Was bending some sheet metal," Sam slurred. "It got away from me, that's all." Sam looked at his arm, seeming to forget the broken glass pointed at Carrie. The thought occurred to her to lunge after it, but her feet were mired in place.

"We'll need to take you to the hospital...get some stitches," Cash said.

Sam took a step backward. He waved the bottle between Carrie and Cash. "No you don't. I'm not going to any damn hospital. And I'm not taking any drug test, either."

Cash held up his hands and advanced. "Sam, Sam. This isn't the way to handle it, my friend." He extended his right palm. "Give me the bottle, Sam. You don't want to hurt anyone. I know you don't."

Sam straightened his arm, waving the jagged glass near Carrie's face. "You don't know squat, Cash Cunningham. Ever since *she*—" he pointed the sharp edge at Carrie again and she instinctively fell back a step "—since she turned your brain to mush, you don't run this company anymore." He turned on Carrie and shouted. "*She* does. Her and her damn manual."

Carrie felt her legs shake. She wanted to rub her upper arms, to find some heat in her veins, but she was afraid to move a hair. Though surrounded by workers, she had a sudden feeling of isolation, as though a giant chasm had opened between everyone else and herself.

"Besides . . . ," Sam stumbled and nearly fell. "I need something for the pain . . . that's all . . . didn't mean to drop it . . ." He looked at the broken bottle as if noticing its condition for the first time.

"Sam—" Cash inched forward "—I'm taking you to the hospital. Right now. Come on." Cash placed a hand on Sam's shoulder and gently turned him toward the open overhead doors behind them, easing him away slowly. Sam staggered through the open space as though it were two feet wide instead of twenty, but didn't resist. When they were far from the crowd, Cash took the bottle from Sam, dumped the remaining contents on the ground, then tossed the empty fifth into a Dumpster.

The adrenaline that had held Carrie together seeped out of her, leaving her nauseous and shaking. The fresh bandages she'd tried to apply earlier lay in a sodden pile on the floor. Shards of glass glistened a few feet away beneath Sam's open locker.

With her breathing still labored, she watched Cash guide Sam into the passenger seat of the Mercedes and buckled him in with great care. A co-worker ran up to them with a clean towel, and then ran back inside.

Cash wrapped Sam's arm, shut the door, then turned and faced Carrie. Their eyes met for one, long, searing moment. In that short space of time she saw pain, sadness...and an overwhelming relief that she was out of harm's way. Something else flashed between them before he walked to the driver's side, but it wasn't anything she could describe at the moment. Later maybe when she was alone.

The grapevine was fast and vivid. For the next few hours, work was only toyed with as one more snippet, one more detail was passed along. The prevailing feeling seemed that of shock and sadness. No one wanted to believe Sam could have acted the way he had.

Carrie sat behind her desk with her head nestled in her folded arms, which rested atop a pile of extra manuals. Her bloodied blouse had been rinsed as clean as she could get it, and now she wore a company T-shirt, her bare arms covered with goose bumps.

She'd gone over and over it again in her head, trying to rationalize her actions earlier this morning. Someone—she didn't who—had called her, asked her to get down to the shop, there was a problem. Then he'd hung up. Another call had come right on its heels. *He's been drinking. You know what the policy says. He'll have to be tested, won't he? He's—we're—not safe anymore.*

Cash hadn't arrived yet. She'd had no choice but to go.

Carrie vaguely heard the door open and the whoosh of the cushion as someone sat in the chair in front of her. Still she didn't move or look up. Every part of her felt numb. All but her heart, and it was so heavy with regret and sadness it paralyzed her.

"Are you okay?" Cash asked in a husky voice. He sounded as bad as she felt. She heard him stand and walk to her. In the next seconds he was on his knees beside her, swiveling her chair toward him, her head and arms reluctantly giving way to the motion.

She took her time looking at him, afraid what she might see in his eyes. Beyond that, she was more worried she'd throw her arms around his neck and cry. It wasn't the crying that would matter. It was the touching. She didn't think she could have his arms around her now and deny what she'd been feeling for some time.

Cash lifted her chin with his finger and she saw that the warm blue was back in his eyes. "I—I'm *really* sorry, Cash." She jerked her hand toward the manuals on her desk. "In theory it was good... but look what I did." She bit her lip to keep from crying.

"Carrie, listen to me." He lifted her chin again. "This problem was a long time in coming. If anyone's to blame it's me... for ignoring the signs all these months." He stood and walked to the glass wall. "All I could think of was building the business, making more money. The faster the better. Clean up the mess later." He turned back to her.

"Now I have a real mess." He cocked his head and studied her a moment. "I could use some help if you're up to it... or I could take you home and we can deal with this tomorrow. Your choice."

As exhausted as she felt, she knew action would probably help. She tried to stand, but dropped back into her chair. "Where do we start?"

He closed the distance between them with two fast strides and placed his warm hands on her shoulders. She gazed up at him, watching his lips, willing them closer. But when they moved it was only to form a sad smile.

"Stay here and I'll get you some coffee." He started for the door, then stopped. "No. You like tea, don't you?"

Since when had he noticed? "Y-yes. N-no. I mean... I like both. Right now I think I could use some strong black coffee. Thank you."

By the time he returned she'd made another trip to the rest room, splashed cold water on her face and removed the last traces of streaked mascara. She almost felt human when he handed her the steaming mug and sat down.

"We need to call a staff meeting, don't you think?" Carrie sipped and nodded, grateful that Cash was the one spewing out the words for a change. "First, I think I should start by telling them we're adding an employee assistance program just as soon as it can be arranged . . . next week if possible."

"Yes," she said between sips. "And everyone who was present this morning should have a chance to talk with a counselor right away . . . get it out."

Cash watched her a moment before replying. "I agree . . . which means you, too."

"I'm okay. I just—" Cash folded his arms. "Y-yes. You're right."

Before he continued, his eyebrows shot up as if he'd just witnessed a miracle. "After they have a few minutes to digest that and to ask whatever questions they have, then I'll tell them about . . . about Sam."

The look on Cash's face made her wonder if more had happened, but before she could ask, he pressed on. "It's probably best to give them the abbreviated version." His words trailed off as he leaned his elbows on his knees and stared at the floor.

"Do you think it would help to tell me about it first?"

His head came up and he held her gaze. His face looked ravaged by the events of the day. More than anything she wanted to go to him and press it between her breasts, stroke his dark hair and assure him all would be well.

But she couldn't, of course. She knew the signal it would send, if not now, then later. Today, of all days, she had to follow the rules.

Employer, employee . . . employer, employee . . . She kept chanting the words in her head, reminding herself of the boundaries, till finally Cash let out a long, loud breath, leaned back and told her the rest of the story.

"As they were wheeling him away in the hospital he hollered at me all the way down the hall. He said he'd never sign any—well, I'll leave out the expletives—any consent form to be tested for drugs." Cash shook his head. "It's a wonder the nurses weren't intoxicated, breathing the same air he expelled." He stood and walked behind the chair, grasping the back of it with both hands. "Anyway... he also said he quit, that I could take the job and— I think you get the picture."

Carrie pushed out of her chair and moved closer, keeping a safe distance. "Are you going to accept his resignation?"

"What choice do I have? According to the manual, if he refuses to sign a consent form so we can have him tested, that's grounds for immediate dismissal. If he hadn't quit, I would've been forced to fire him. Either that or send a message to all the other employees that the rules only apply to some."

"I'm so sorry, Cash." Her words seemed inadequate. A heavy silence fell over the room, and neither of them moved nor spoke for the longest time.

"Carrie... if you could gather everyone up in the conference room, I'd really appreciate it. The sooner we get this over with the better."

She merely nodded and leaned against the back of her desk.

"Let me organize my thoughts and I'll be right down." He looked at her one last time, in the same searing way as when he'd stood by his car earlier this morning. "When the meeting's over I plan to send everyone home for the day." He paused a moment. "Can you stay for just a little longer?"

"Yes."

He held her gaze another few seconds, then turned and walked away.

When the last employee had left the room after the meeting, Cash dropped wearily into the front-row chair next to Carrie. "Have you ever seen such a sad group of people?" he asked.

"You did well. They're still upset, that's all. But you did very well," she repeated.

"You think so?" He seemed genuinely interested in her opinion. Somewhere in this disaster a partnership had been forged. It no longer felt like *his* plan or *her* idea. Now it was theirs—a feeling that warmed as well as frightened her.

"Yes, I do," she finally answered. "They seemed most interested in the EAP and had lots of good questions. And telling them that Sam no longer worked here was enough for now. Some of his cronies will find out the rest later, and everyone will know. But that's okay. You only said positive things—that he'd been a longtime, valued employee, that it was an unfortunate loss. There are a lot of employers who would have forgotten to say those things at a time like this." She was proud of him, but she couldn't quite add that.

Cash exhaled loudly. "Mind if we change the subject?"

Carrie nodded, purposefully keeping her gaze straight ahead, away from the man beside her.

"Peggy's really been after me about a Christmas party again, and since you've started working here I almost decided it might be a good idea." Cash slid down in his chair and crossed his ankles. "Now I don't know. I think we should forget it."

Carrie turned in her chair, feeling the first burst of energy all day. "Oh, no, Cash. That's exactly what we need— a Christmas party! That's perfect."

He returned her enthusiasm with a small smile. "You're perfect." Quickly he looked away, and she thought she saw some pink just below his hair line. "I—I mean...you're just what Cunningham Construction has needed for a long time." He stood and shook both legs and walked to the podium for his notes. His back to her he said, "Since we're leaving for San Francisco Wednesday, maybe you could whip up invitations tomorrow. I'd like the party to be held somewhere other than here— Maybe my house, a week from Saturday—"

"I'll help Peggy arrange the catering." Carrie picked up her own notes and started for the door.

Never looking up, he asked, "Are you sure you don't want me to drive you home?"

"No. No, really. I—I'm fine."

With rounded shoulders he walked toward the exit without meeting her steady gaze. "Okay, then. See you tomorrow."

Carrie stood when he was out of sight. Feeling as though she were sleepwalking, she went to the rest room one last time. She'd make sure Cash had time to get his coat and be gone before she did the same. If she ran into him one more time, if he asked to drive her home one more time, she knew she'd say yes. And then what? Would he walk her upstairs to her apartment? Could they resist seeking comfort in each other's arms? How far would it go before—

She looked in the mirror and saw too many answers.

Eventually she made the slow descent to the parking lot and let Woodie take her home. An hour and a half later, curled under an afghan on her sofa, she let go of the tears that had been lodged at the back of her throat all day.

Eleven

Tuesday was the quietest day Carrie had ever experienced at work. With Cash's permission, she played Christmas music over the sound system, hoping to pump a little cheer into everyone's day. Instead it seemed to spread melancholy. After lunch she turned it off.

Sam was well liked. In spite of yesterday's events, everyone knew Sam was a talented, hard worker, and ever loyal to Cunningham Construction. Not to mention that he had a family to support and Christmas wasn't anyone's favorite time of year to become unemployed.

In her heart Carrie knew this wasn't her fault. Sam had been a walking grenade. It was just that she felt as if she was the one who'd pulled the pin.

Tuesday night she packed a bag for San Francisco without the enthusiasm she'd first felt when Cash invited her. Wednesday morning she threw it on Woodie's passenger seat and drove north to Monterey.

At nine o'clock Cash stood in her doorway, looking as though he hadn't slept in days. "I'm not getting much done here.... Thought about heading out early. How long before you can be ready to go?"

Carrie turned off her computer, grabbed her purse out of the bottom drawer and stood. "Now."

That brought a small smile to his haggard face. "I'll be right down. Wait at your car and I'll pull alongside and load your luggage." He rapped on the door jamb twice and then left.

Carrie made a quick stop at the ladies' room, tried forking some shape into her tangled curls, gave up and took the elevator downstairs. The lights on the tree shimmered and danced as though there weren't a problem in the world. Carrie stopped and looked up at the star she'd anchored on top just a week ago today. Everyone had been so happy then, full of hope and promise that this would be the harmonious workplace they'd wished for but hadn't had. She let her gaze travel down the twenty feet of branches, trying to remember who had brought which decoration.

Suddenly she stepped back and squared her shoulders, speaking aloud in the empty atrium. "Well, S...you started this mission of merriment. Now you had better finish it." Looking at her watch, she dashed out the door and to her car where Cash waited.

Yep. Problems were simply challenges in disguise. Before she returned here Friday, she'd strip away the layers and find the solution. Cunningham Construction was going to be the best place to work—whatever it took.

She threw her bag in Cash's open trunk and jumped into his passenger seat. She smiled at his puzzled face and almost laughed. "We're ahead of schedule, right?"

"Right," he said, suspicion creasing his forehead.

"Well, then...why don't we take the Seventeen Mile Drive on our way?" It was a cool but clear day. The scenic route around Monterey Peninsula had always been one of her favorites, one she'd neglected for too long.

"It's not exactly on the way." He studied her a moment, then gave her a weak smile. "But I think it can be arranged." He revved the engine and sped off.

A few minutes later when they neared the entrance to the tour, Carrie said, "I'll even pay the admission fee." She dug in her purse, but Cash stilled her hand.

"You think I'm that much of a Scrooge?"

She looked over at him, bit her top lip, then stared at the space above his head. Cash made a harrumphing sound before paying the attendant.

Carrie studied the brochure given to them as they drove on. "I know we can't spend all morning here, so what shall we see?"

"It's entirely up to you. I see a lot of it every week. Your choice."

She turned on him, surprised such things even interested him. "Really? Do you live near here?"

"Just a few blocks away...in Pacific Grove."

He seemed more relaxed than when they'd left, and she was glad they'd come. She was tempted to ask him to drive by his house, but...

"You'll see it at the party a week from Saturday," he said with a smug look on his face.

"And what makes you think—"

He interrupted her. "Carrie, if there's one thing you are it's transparent."

Really! She folded her arms and stared straight ahead. Well, she'd see about that. She'd think of something right now that he'd never guess in a million years. Instantly her thoughts went to the St. Francis Hotel. *They were dining in one of the finer restaurants.... A trio played romantic music in the corner.... He asked her to dance....*

She could feel the heat creep up her neck to her cheeks, and she nearly cursed aloud. More than transparent, she suddenly felt naked. Out of the corner of her eye she saw Cash glance at her and heard a small chuckle. Looking out her side window, she reined in her overactive imagination and said, "I'd like to see Bird Rock, Seal Rock and The Lone Cypress . . . and anything else you think we have time for."

"Coming right up," he said, as she continued staring out the window.

They pulled off the road and from the car watched the birds and seals lounging on their large rocky areas. Carrie spotted a family of sea otters and smiled at their playful antics. After a time they drove on. Deer clustered here and there on the golf course to their left, confidently lounging on the fairway, knowing they were safe from predators. When they arrived at The Lone Cypress and the car rolled to a stop, Carrie got out and stepped carefully over the rocks, stopping where the path began. The twisted old Monterey cypress had practically become synonymous with the peninsula, inspiring an awe she could never quite put into words.

"This is my favorite spot," Cash whispered over her shoulder, and she nearly jumped. She could feel his breath on her neck. The pounding of another wave against the granite cliff matched the force of her heartbeat. His hand lay gently on her shoulder, and the tree blurred in front of her when he spoke again.

"It's over two hundred and fifty years old...some say as much as five hundred. Can you imagine the stories it could tell?"

"May-maybe we should get going." She stepped forward and his hand fell away. When she glanced over her shoulder, she met his eyes and saw a glimpse of vulnerability that made her shudder. Quickly she turned back, her defenses feeling as fragile as the aged tree that clung precariously to the rocky promontory in front of her. Another high-breaking wave washed over its gnarled trunk, and she heard his footsteps retreating toward the car.

Three days and two nights. Out of town. With Cash—this man who loves cypress trees and who knows what else.

She walked back, slid into the car and shut the door behind her. Why couldn't he be the cold, heartless tightwad
she'd met last month? She pictured his impersonal, sterile
office, the empty atrium she'd first seen. Was there a home
in Pacific Grove that could possibly look like his office? She
doubted it. Mostly the homes there were Victorians built as
summer retreats, many converted to cozy bed-and-breakfast
spots.

And this other Cash lived in one of them.

They were back on Highway 1 headed north and he
hadn't said a word since the tour. It was almost as though
he were in a world of his own. She slouched in her seat and
decided to enjoy the silence.

At Santa Cruz they headed east and sped along the freeway till they reached 280, then he turned north again. After
more than an hour of nothing but the radio, she couldn't
help wonder what he was thinking. Sure, he was upset over
Sam. So was she, and everyone else. Yet *upset* didn't seem
to describe his darker mood. Back at The Lone Cypress,
he'd appeared warmer than usual. Then in a flash he had
become withdrawn, virtually ignoring her ever since. And
for the past half hour, whenever she glanced over, there was
an angry, even hostile set to his jaw. It had to be more than
Sam that was eating at him. She'd seen this look before. It
was as if he were battling some private demon and was about
to smash his fist through something. Anything.

They passed the exit for Stanford University and she knew
she couldn't remain silent another second. She exhaled
loudly, then looked over.

"I heard you graduated from Stanford?"

"That's right." He didn't look at her, nor did his posture
relax. If anything, he seemed more edgy.

What was the big deal? Everyone at work knew the story
about how he put himself through college.

Lost for another opening, Carrie turned her attention to
the scenery. She spotted a cable car and smiled. She loved

this city and nothing grumpy old Scrooge could say was going to ruin her short stay here. She folded her arms across her chest as they turned up Market Street for Union Square. But before long, she tried drawing him out again.

"You know... over the next couple days, you'll learn so much about EAPs, you'll probably feel more like an attorney than a contractor."

"Just like Brian, huh?" he snapped.

She whipped around in her seat. "How did you know Brian was an attorney?"

"I saw him at the club last night, working out. A friend of mine knows him and told me."

"What else did this friend tell you?"

"That Brian was engaged to a 'real hot number,' to use his words." Cash shot her a glance.

"Well, you can tell your friend he's out of touch. I ended that relationship months ago." She wiggled her left hand near the steering wheel. "Do you think a successful attorney would let his fiancé walk around without a rock on her finger?"

Cash glanced at her hand and she saw a shadow of doubt cross his handsome features. She dropped her hand in her lap and looked back at the cable car, which had stopped just ahead near the parking entrance to the St. Francis. Her breath caught in her throat as she took in the sights of the city. She couldn't stay angry with him if she tried. There was so much to see and do. Thankfully, the workshop coordinator had built in free time. Today's introductory session only ran from two till five. Then nothing till tomorrow.

Cash pulled into the lot behind a long row of cabs and a stretch limousine. He reached into his back pocket. "Here's my credit card. If you want to go ahead and check us in, I'll bring in our bags and meet you in the lobby."

It didn't take a second invitation. Carrie took the card and stepped out of the car, breathing in the crisp December air, welcoming the space between them, if only for a while. She strode directly toward the registration counter on the right and found an open clerk. No sooner had the necessary papers been signed and key cards handed over than she spotted Cash walking toward her, a bag in each hand. Her stomach did another flip-flop. He was such a handsome sight. He walked tall, cool and confident. A few strands of his nearly black hair had scattered across his forehead, making him look more relaxed and casual than she knew was the case.

Who was she to talk about relaxed and casual? She wasn't sure she'd been either since the day she'd met this man. Now she was going to try to fix that by spending a couple of days and nights in one of the most romantic hotels in one of the most romantic cities in the world.

Smart move, S. Real smart.

She walked side by side with him to the bank of elevators, stepped into the first one that opened, then stared at the numbers over the door as they made their ascent. They walked down the long hall and found their rooms—next to each other, of course. She used the card in the first room and walked in, tossing her shoulder bag on the king-size bed.

Behind her Cash deposited her suitcase and said, "I have a few calls to make. Why don't we meet at the conference registration desk at 1:45?"

Carrie walked to the window and looked out at Union Square. "Sounds fine to me."

"Fine," he said, shutting the door behind him when he left.

Fine. Just fine. Her stomach growled, reminding her she hadn't eaten since she'd left home. Maybe she should order room service. She smiled a wicked smile. Maybe the most expensive thing on the menu. Wouldn't that get his pulse jumping!

She opened her suitcase, hung a few things up and put the rest in a drawer. After a quick change into slacks and a sweater, she freshened her face and studied her wild head of curls. The perm had settled down a little, but not much. She dampened her fingers and scrunched a few frizzy areas, then shrugged and left the room. Room service had sounded fun, but she needed space and, if time allowed, a good brisk walk.

Yep. That would do the trick. Before two o'clock she'd have her head back on straight and remember that Cash was simply her boss.

All the way down the hall, then down the elevator, through lunch and a short walk to Neiman Marcus and back, she chanted the reminder in her head, matching the rhythm of her movements. *He's only my employer.... I need this job.... He's only my employer.... It's against the rules.... He's only my employer.... Keep your cool....*

At precisely 1:45 she approached the registration table and saw him standing in line, his back to her. He'd changed into a blue chambray shirt and jeans—snug-fitting jeans— that hugged his perfectly rounded backside. Hips narrow, shoulders broad. He looked to his left and right, then turned around and spotted her. A small smile lifted one corner of his mouth.

This was going to be harder than she'd thought.

Twelve

Cash stared at the back of the unruly red hair in front of him. How had he allowed himself to get into such a compromising position? He could have attended this conference by himself. He was the one who needed to learn. Carrie could probably teach the class. Whatever he'd been thinking when he made this decision was probably as dangerous as the scent of her perfume filling his nostrils all the way north in the small confines of his car. Even now he found it difficult to concentrate. Her fresh, rosy scent drifted his way whenever she tossed her hair over her shoulder or slid her hand across the back of her neck, rotating it from side to side. He had an urge to reach across the table and massage her shoulders.

Yet somewhere along the way, after the introductions, Cash began to listen to the speaker. He seemed experienced and articulate, with a sense of humor that should make the subject matter at least tolerable. By the looks of the outline in front of him, he had his work cut out for him. *Recruit-*

ing, hiring, testing, training, motivating, keeping. All of it with a legal slant, designed to cover one's backside.

Legal... lawyers. Like Brian.

Brian. Why did he keep coming back to that guy? And why had he felt relieved when Carrie told him the engagement had been over for some time?

Cash was still succumbing to this dangerous line of thought when the class ended at five o'clock and he filed out behind the others.

Down in the lobby, he stopped and looked around. A harp played in the lounge, a few steps up and to the right. It sounded restful and inviting. He noticed Carrie looking wistfully in its direction. Many of the other conference attendees were making their way up the steps, getting acquainted, chatting enthusiastically. Cash headed for the elevators. First he'd get rid of his paperwork, then he'd get his coat and go outside.

The scent of roses was right behind him. She came alongside when he stopped to punch the Up button.

"Feel free to join the others if you'd like." Please! The tension he needed to walk off had less to do with sitting through a few hours of lecture than being with this...this tempting... "I need a little fresh air and exercise," he said, staring at the floral pattern of the carpet.

"Mind if I join you?" she asked, sounding all cheery and excited.

He shot her a not-too-welcoming look. "I was thinking of a brisk walk around Union Square, then eating out somewhere."

She smiled up at him. "Sounds great."

The door slid open and they stepped inside. All this togetherness had to be a mistake. But what was he to do? Tell her he didn't want her company?

In spite of the warning bells ringing in his skull, he knew that was the farthest thing from the truth.

Carrie refrained from slowing her pace around the Square to admire the beautifully decorated windows, doing her best to keep up with Cash's long stride. When he began to slow down, she took in the white bells and holly that adorned streetlights, the animated Santa's workshop in one window and the towering tree that sparkled merrily in the Square's center park. She'd never been here during the holidays, and now she wondered why. She and her father and friends had rarely ventured north, preferring the drive south along the bold cliffs of Big Sur.

When they neared the entrance to the hotel, Carrie spotted another cable car and stopped to catch her breath.

"Why don't we hop one and go down to Fishermans' Wharf? We could eat somewhere with a view of the Bay, maybe take in the Golden Gate Bridge." She saw him stiffen and knew what his answer would be before it came.

"No. I'd prefer to stay around here. Chinatown is within walking distance and I've worked up a good appetite. Haven't you?" He gave her a forced grin that didn't fool her for a second. There was a reason he'd refused the Wharf, and before this night ended she'd know why. There was a lot she didn't know about this man. It was time she learned.

They walked the few blocks in silence, Carrie biting back her curiosity. They found a restaurant with a short line and were seated soon after. Halfway through dinner Carrie set her chopsticks down and picked up her small handleless tea cup. It was time for a little probing.

"So, Cash . . ." He looked up at her without a smile. Did he know what subject she was about to broach? Or was being stuck with her all day and night the source of his angst? Whichever, she wasn't going to stop now. "When you went to Stanford, did you stay on campus or did you live in this area?"

She watched him chew slowly, looking as though he were debating what, if anything, to tell her.

"I stayed in a dorm till my junior year," he said flatly, sending a clear signal that he hoped the subject was now closed.

Huh! Not by a long shot. "And after that?" she asked, smiling at him as though she'd missed the hint.

Cash set the sticks down, leaned back in his chair and eyed her for a moment before speaking. Was this the beginning of a meaningful conversation or the time when he told her to mind her own business?

"I rented the attic of an elderly woman's home in Nob Hill, not far from here." Unexpectedly he smiled, his gaze drifting off to an obviously good memory, and Carrie let out a slow breath.

"That's where it all began—" His face was more relaxed than Carrie thought she'd ever seen. "My love affair with old ladies."

Her shocked expression must have given her away, because he was quick to laugh, then explain.

"That's what they call the Victorian homes—grand old ladies. And that they are." He drank some tea, warming to his subject. "The widow who let the attic to me was struggling to hold on to her home. It was all she could do to pay the utilities and feed herself. I started doing minor repairs for her at first, then things sort of escalated. One summer I caulked and painted the entire exterior, replacing more than a few rotten boards. The next thing I knew I was working from a list—everything from replacing plumbing fixtures to refinishing the hardwood floors. She stopped charging me rent, yet I ended up spending what I saved on materials. But I didn't mind." He drank more tea and eyed Carrie for the first time since starting his story. "It was a labor of love... and it taught me a lot about construction. Most importantly that it was what I wanted to do with my life."

"What was your major?"

"Business." He laughed. "At the time I wished it was architecture, but in the long run it's been an asset... now that I have my own company." He looked off across the room. "I never intended to. I think I would have been happy restoring the old ladies the rest of my life."

"Then how did it happen? I mean...your business?" What started as curiosity had evolved into something else. Now she truly wanted to know what made this man tick. In the deep recesses of her mind she knew this was not a safe detour she'd taken.

"Well, Agnes told her friends about my work, and one at a time they all asked for help. I couldn't keep up with it and finally asked friends for loans so I could hire help, buy materials...all in exchange for a percentage of my profits." He chuckled and shook his head. "I kept raising my prices, hoping to discourage customers, since I was struggling to keep up my studies and the jobs, too. Funny how that works. The higher the value I placed on my time, the more they thought I must be the best man for the job. With the healthy profits I turned, friends starting telling friends and pretty soon I had investors lining up offering me funds. Amazing."

"The Midas touch," she said nodding. Then a light bulb went on in her head. "Is Cash your real name?"

His chuckle was low. "I was born Cass Cunningham and—"

"—and the nickname Cash came from that time." She felt a little smug for having figured it out, but then she realized she was probably the only one at Cunningham Construction who didn't know this story.

"Besides Sam, I don't know if anyone at work knows how I came to be called Cash."

His revelation and the way he was holding her gaze did something to her chest. She fought to catch her breath, hoping he didn't notice. The quickest way to find oxygen was to bypass personal conversation, she thought. Then she heard herself ask, "Before college...did you live in San Francisco?"

The smile disappeared from his eyes and he looked away. "Yes."

They sat in stony silence while the waiter cleared their table and returned with fortune cookies a moment later.

Way to go, S. She'd pressed too far. Now the conversation had stalled and she couldn't think of a graceful way to jump-start it. She stared at the fortune cookies but decided against taking one—just in case it told her to stop prying.

"We lived in Pacific Heights," he said eventually. "My...*parents*...and myself." There was no mistaking the animosity in his phrasing, Carrie thought. Cash leaned his elbows on the table, steepled his fingers and looked off into some dark area of his life. "My father was a dentist and my mother...well, my mother planned parties...one after the other." The way he spoke, it was almost as if he were alone. "When she wasn't drunk she was either high on prescription drugs or out like a light. At first Dad made excuses for her. Eventually he just gave up and joined her."

Cash gazed at Carrie briefly, sending her a searing look that surely revealed far more than he intended. It was obvious he had no love for his mother. She wondered if all women were guilty of something in his eyes.

He picked up the tab left by the waiter, removed sufficient bills from his wallet, then stood. "Mind if we head back?" He came around to Carrie's side of the table without waiting for an answer and pulled out her chair.

She looked up at him a moment, trying to think of the right thing to say, but he was staring at the floor and obviously just wanted to leave. At the very least, she could say she was sorry, but she sensed no response was the right one for now.

They were nearly back to the St. Francis when he spoke again. "About the Wharf...maybe you'll find a group going down there tomorrow. Don't feel like you have to stay with me."

She remembered gossip at work about a boating accident. Was that it? Had his parents drowned near the Wharf? Cash held the door open and she passed in front of him, afraid to look up.

Her and her big mouth. Snooping where she had no business. Still, why had he been so forthcoming with the

information? He'd always seemed such a private person before. Now, riding the elevator to their floor, she sensed he
wanted to tell her more. She wished he'd open up to her, but
she wouldn't pry again.

They stepped out of the elevator and Carrie matched
Cash's slow steps. It was as though she could hear the de-
bate in his head. She eyed him without turning her head.
Pain and need etched his handsome features.

When they arrived at her door, she took her time finding
her key card in her purse, hoping he'd tell her more. Finally
he leaned a shoulder against the wall and let out a long
breath.

"Great company tonight, huh?"

She fingered the key card in her hand, feeling his gaze on
her. "I'm just glad you felt comfortable talking to me,
Cash," she said softly. She looked up and noticed the lines
had disappeared from his face, but the pain lingered behind his eyes.

"Mind if I ask a question?" he asked, a shy smile curv-
ing his lips.

Carrie shook her head, unable to look away from those
sad blue eyes.

"You never told me about your mother... or would you
rather not?"

She closed her eyes for a moment, unable to say anything, but then the words came rushing out. "It was just
before my fifth birthday. Mom got hit by a car—"

He stepped forward and placed a warm hand on her
shoulder, and she shivered. "Carrie, I'm sorry. I didn't
mean to—"

"I don't mind telling you, but it's not a short story." She
smiled up at him. "It's a beautiful one, though."

"Beautiful?"

"Yes. Beautiful... even quite miraculous. W-would you
like to come in a minute?"

He looked at the door as if it were a portal through which
he shouldn't pass, but he took her key card and inserted it
in the slot. "For a few minutes."

She walked directly to the round table in front of the window and sat in one of the two chairs, shrugging out of her coat when she was settled. Cash took the other chair, unbuttoning his coat but leaving it on. She looked at the bed, then back to Cash, trying her hardest to concentrate on the reason he was here.

"The—the young man who was driving was a good kid, but his parents had just told him they were divorcing. He took off in the car, angry with the world. The cops said Steve had to be doing at least eighty. There were skid marks all the way down the street."

"Steve? You make it sound like he's a friend of the family's."

Carrie smiled. "He is now." She saw the stunned expression on Cash's face. "It's really quite remarkable." She kicked off her shoes and tucked her legs up under her. "At first my father was so grief stricken he could barely function. But later, Steve's parents came to our house to talk to Dad." She could picture it as if it were yesterday. Although she'd been only five, the day had made an indelible impression. "I answered the door that night and Dad heard them introduce themselves. I'd never seen him so angry before. He came charging to the door, swearing at them, telling them they had a lot of nerve coming. Then Steve's mom started to cry and his dad kept saying it was all his fault, that he should be punished instead of his son. Then he started crying, too. It was awful." Carrie pulled a tissue from the box on the table beside her and blew her nose.

"Carrie...you don't have to—"

"No, no. I want to." She dabbed at her eyes and continued. "My dad calmed down and asked them to come in. They were there for a long time, and Dad made me go to bed. I didn't want to, but I didn't understand a lot of what was being said, anyway. In time I came to understand everything." Including the fact that she had the best dad in the whole world.

"Steve was about to enter the seminary when his parents dropped their bomb on him. Not only were they divorcing, but they were having financial difficulties and they told him there wouldn't be enough money for the seminary. Dad didn't make any promises that night, but a few days later he went and talked to the prosecuting attorney. Steve never went to trial, but he did go to the seminary." She eyed Cash through a sheen of fresh tears, her heart bursting with love and pride for her father.

"Dad put him through. Today he's a very well respected priest in the Midwest . . . and his parents recently celebrated their fiftieth wedding anniversary."

Cash held her gaze for the longest moment before he spoke.

"I wish I could meet your father," he whispered.

"So do I." *Oh, so do I, Cash. He would love you just as—*

Carrie popped out of her chair. "We have a long day tomorrow. Maybe we should—"

Cash stood at the same time. "Yes, yes. I should be going." He walked ahead of her to the door. With his hand on the knob, he turned sideways and opened his mouth to speak. But then he turned the handle and stepped out into the hall. "Good night, Carrie."

"Good night, Cash."

Thirteen

At six the next morning Cash sat on a bench in the Square and stared at the lights of the towering tree. It reminded him of the one in his atrium. Carrie's little project. He gathered his coat around him to ward off the cold morning air, knowing as he did it that something else had caused the chill coursing through him.

He'd been up since five. All through the night, memories of his parents had swirled in his head, mixed with snippets of Carrie's story about her dad. When all thoughts centered around Carrie he'd given up on sleep and headed for the shower.

Carrie. What was he to do about Carrie?

His own damn policies prohibited dating her. Yet how much longer could they work side by side without more. Much more? He shook his head, remembering how beautiful she'd looked sitting in her room, her face aglow with pride as she told her incredible story. With a father like that, it was no wonder she was such a happy and giving person.

There had been a time when he'd thought his father was a hero too...before the booze and pills...before there was so much to forgive.

Cash pushed off the bench and started walking. As problematic as his feelings toward Carrie had become, he preferred thinking of her rather than his parents any day. A few quick strides and the image of her silhouetted near the window, with the bed close behind her, reappeared. He had wanted to lie beside her, hold her, let her warmth seep into his cold and empty soul.

Several blocks from the hotel, he stopped and swore under his breath. He had to remember why he was in San Francisco. There were employees at home who counted on him. He had responsibilities that had to come first. He checked his watch and, with a droop in his shoulders, headed back.

At five Cash looked over the heads of the milling crowd and found the short red beacon talking animatedly to a captive audience. He smiled and crossed to her. He hadn't seen her since they'd divvied up the schedule of workshops this morning, and now he was eager to tell her what he'd learned.

As he neared her, he saw the smiles on the crowd around her. Amazing. She had friends within minutes of entering a room. Something akin to pride rippled under his sweater as he neared her.

Carrie waved to her companions and raced toward him. "Wasn't it wonderful? Do you want to go for a walk and talk? Or should we wait till dinner?" She looked over her shoulder at the others who were walking up the steps to the lounge. "Or maybe—"

"Whoa. Slow down." He reached for her elbow, then had second thoughts. He stuck his hands in his pockets. "Last time I heard, it was about fifty degrees outside. Let's get our coats and take a slow walk...look in the store windows."

She spun away from him and was halfway to the elevators before he stopped grinning and joined her. "I met an interesting EAP provider today," he said when he caught up with her. "I think they might help us solve some of our problems—"

"Performance Consultants?" she asked, sounding sure of herself.

"Well . . . yes." Why did he always feel as if he was running to keep up with this little redhead? And why did it amuse him instead of make him angry the way it used to?

"PC is terrific. It's one of those I told you about." She sprang out of the elevator and practically skipped down the hall with unbridled enthusiasm.

"Wait a minute. I'll be right back." When he stepped inside his room and shrugged into his coat, he laughed aloud. They could have stayed home and Carrie could have taught him everything he'd just learned today. He stopped a moment and thought about it. She probably knew that was true. But would he have listened to her? Or been as convinced that he was doing what was best for his company? His employees?

Probably not. He grinned and met her in the hall.

Their trip around the Square was a leisurely one with stops here and there to admire decorations and alluring displays of high-priced merchandise.

"I'm glad you've decided on Performance Consultants," Carrie said, studying a dark green sequined gown in the window of Saks Fifth Avenue.

"Any idea how long before we could offer something to our employees?" he asked, strolling alongside her when she moved on.

"Next week," she said, matter-of-factly. "I talked to Rich— " she glanced at Cash and kept walking "—at lunchtime. Just asked some hypothetical questions."

Cash laughed aloud. "You mean you haven't signed a contract yet?"

Carrie stopped and faced him, looking insulted. "Why, of course not. You're the president. This is your decision."

He bit back a smile.

"What's so funny?" she asked, tilting her chin higher.

He stared at her full lips, and this morning's dreams returned with a vengeance. He balled his fists in his coat pockets and did a slow ninety-degree turn. "Mind if we have dinner at the hotel tonight?"

"Mind! The St. Francis is so beautiful . . . especially with all the poinsettias and lights."

Cash quickened his steps, lecturing himself with each long stride back to the hotel. A quick dinner, more business talk. Keep it light. Neutral. A couple more hours and he could be in his room. Alone. Banging his head against the wall if need be, but safe.

And away from this off-limits temptation.

Over dim candlelight Cash read PC's sample contract, discussing a few points with Carrie from time to time. They decided who would attend what tomorrow morning and that Cash would make a point of finding PC's representatives about sending a formal contract immediately.

Now they drank cappuccino and listened to "I'll Be Home for Christmas" drifting softly from the piano player in the corner.

All he had to do was sign the tab and escort her to her room.

The tune ended and another one began. The waiter stopped at their table and asked if they were interested in refills.

With her cup to her lips, Carrie eyed Cash.

"Yes," he said, holding her gaze.

After the waiter returned and left again, Cash ventured a little farther into the woods, a part of him knowing before the first word was uttered where this path would lead. "I've been thinking about the story you told me last night."

Carrie smiled at him, candlelight giving her an angelic glow.

"How do you think your father was able to forgive those people?"

She set her cup down and gave him a small wave of the hand. "Oh, that part is easy to understand. My mother," she said, and leaned back in her chair.

"Your mother?" He sipped his cappuccino and eyed her patiently.

"Yes." A wistful expression smoothed out the dimples on either side of her mouth. "I cried a lot at first ... especially at bedtime, when she usually read me a story. After a while, when Dad felt a little better, he started reading to me. Eventually we forgot about books and he made up the most wonderful stories." She stopped suddenly and looked at Cash. "Am I boring you?"

"No. Not at all. But if this is making you sad—"

"No," she said, and flashed him a warm smile. "I love talking about my parents."

If only he could say the same.

"Anyway, he told me Mama was an angel in heaven and that unlike before—when I could actually see her—now she saw every move I made ... that I could talk to her without opening my mouth. All I had to do was think the words and she would hear me."

A lone tear trailed down Carrie's cheek, and Cash found it hard to swallow. He also found it hard not to reach across their narrow table and brush the tear away. He twisted his cup in both hands instead.

Carrie sniffed and ran a finger under her eye. "Those stories became such a part of my life that when Steve's parents came to visit that one night and I was sent to bed ... well, I just snuggled under the covers and talked to Mama. I asked her what we should do to make Steve's mama and daddy stop crying. And she told me." Carrie picked up her mug and drank slowly.

"The next morning, Dad didn't want to hear my story. But that night, when he tucked me in, he listened with his heart and he knew what Mama wanted him to do."

Cash looked up at the ceiling and cleared the mist that curtained his eyes. After a moment he drank more of the lukewarm liquid in his cup, washing down the obstruction in his throat.

For what seemed an eternity, they didn't speak. Cash could feel Carrie's eyes on him and he knew with certainty what she was thinking. She was trying to say something about forgiveness, letting go, and it was aimed at him. If only his parents' tragedy had had such a positive outcome. But what could he tell her? All their deaths had done was make him angry. And broke. And homeless. At the time, the list had seemed endless. Now it seemed pointless to rehash it all.

Yet he could hear the words taking shape in his head, almost as though they had a will of their own. He didn't want to talk about this. He never had before. Something was tugging at him, reaching deep into places he'd rather not go.

They were approaching her room, and still neither had spoken. Back at the table, Carrie had been so sure Cash was about to tell her the rest of his story, but then he'd signed the tab and they'd left.

At the door she turned to say good-night, but he leaned a shoulder against the wall, just as he had done last night. She wanted to invite him in, yet she couldn't. Watching him leave last night had been difficult enough. She didn't know if she had the strength for it again.

Slowly she pocketed the key and looked at the carpet, eager for his words yet fearful of the consequences. An eerie sense of foreboding permeated the space between them. A line was being crossed, and they both knew it.

"It was an overcast spring day...just before my high school graduation. The three of us were sailing the Bay alone for a change." Cash laughed sardonically. "Planning a party, of course."

Carrie braved a look upward. She watched as he turned his back to the wall, tucked his hands behind his waist and

stared at some unknown spot in front of him. A part of her
wanted to say it was okay, he didn't have to finish. Another
part knew he wanted to, wondered if he ever had.

"It started to get dark...and then the rain came. I told
Dad we'd better head for shore, and he agreed. Mom said,
'Just one more drink.'"

Cash looked up, and Carrie felt his pain. Desperately she
wanted to touch his cheek, to stroke away the lines around
his mouth, the sadness that tugged his eyelids lower. But she
didn't move. She tried not to make a sound when she
breathed.

"When we went over—"

She watched him swallow, then tilt his head back till it
touched the wall.

"I kept diving and diving. It was so dark." His voice was
rusty, and he was fighting for control. "When there was
nothing left to hang on to, I swam for shore." His breathing was labored now. Carrie stepped forward and took his
hand. "It was days before they—"

She laced her fingers through his and squeezed hard,
moving closer to his side. When he didn't speak, she rested
her cheek against his rigid arm and began stroking it with
her free hand. She watched his chest swelling and contracting, till finally his breathing slowed and the tension seemed
to ebb.

"One of my speakers today was a psychologist who works
in substance abuse."

Carrie kept stroking his arm, not leaving his side. If she
moved, he might stop talking. But she knew that wasn't the
only reason she clung to him. The warmth of his hand
spread up her arm.

"I can't tell you how many times over the years I've heard
it's an illness...that such people need help, not scorn." He
turned sideways again but didn't let go of her hand. "Yet
today...in context with everything else...I believed it."

Carrie lifted their locked fingers to her chest, bringing him a step closer. She traced the veins on the back of his hand, keeping her gaze locked on her free-flowing finger.

"I've been so angry, Carrie . . . for so many years."

She nodded, not looking up, afraid to break his stride.

"I . . . I can't let this happen again—" He paused, and she lifted her gaze to meet his.

"To one of my employees or their families. Not if I can help it. Already there's Sam."

He stared at their hands and tightened his hold. The spaces on either side of her mother's pearl ring began to hurt. Still she didn't move.

"Today—listening to that speaker—I couldn't help but wonder what would've happened if my dad worked for a company that had a policy like ours. Maybe one of his partners would have forced him to go to their EAP when his performance started slipping." He looked into her eyes, seeming more naked and vulnerable than she ever could have imagined him being. "Carrie . . . it might have saved their lives."

She held his intense gaze, a sudden thickness gobbling up the air around them. It felt as though someone were pushing on her back, gently, nudging her closer and closer. She inched forward, not feeling her feet move. Had he closed the distance between them or had she?

She tilted her head back farther to hold his steady gaze. He let go of her hand and she felt his fingers slide down her arm. Then his hand was in the pocket of her coat. A moment later, the key was in the door.

He stepped over the threshold and reached for her hand again. She gave it to him knowingly, feeling shy. He'd already asked with his eyes. And she knew she'd already answered.

They walked to the window, where the lights of the city washed over them. She could see the turmoil on his face, yet instead of doubting herself, she felt his hesitation drawing her nearer. Of its own volition her hand reached out and touched his stubbled cheek. A moan passed his lips as he stepped closer. His swollen flesh pressed against her belly, proving what she already knew. With both hands she smoothed away his wrinkled brow, her fingertips memorizing each swell and indentation of his face, savoring a view that till this moment had seemed locked behind an impenetrable wall.

His hands trailed down her arms with such a possessive intimacy that Carrie shuddered beneath his touch. He set her away from him and for a moment she thought he had changed his mind. Then he removed her coat and tossed it on the chair behind him, his own joining hers seconds later.

Another bridge had been crossed. She knew several more remained, but she was in no hurry. This wasn't a night for shedding things quickly, neither clothes nor reserves. This was a night to treasure. Every second. Every heartbeat.

Slowly Cash pulled the sweater over her head, then found the small hook at the front of her bra. With exquisite tenderness he slid one strap at a time down her bare shoulders, his gaze finally lowering to her exposed breasts. Those long, graceful fingers she'd admired so often began playing her like a finely tuned instrument. They gently traced the outer swell of her breasts before finding their centers, puckering the skin to full arousal.

With a moan of her own, she began working on the buttons of his shirt till he shrugged out of it. She pulled his T-shirt from his pants, sliding her hands beneath it and over the hard planes of his chest. Except for fleeting moments, his gaze remained riveted on hers.

Somewhere in her haze the word *boss* penetrated the remnants of logical thought, but she quickly dismissed it. This person standing in front of her wasn't her boss now. He was a caring and vulnerable man—one who needed her gentle, healing touch—to his body and his heart. Why she knew this with such certainty seemed of little significance. She knew it. And for now it was all that mattered.

Still watching his face, she undid his buckle and found the zipper. Its slow descent contrasted with their quickened breathing. She studied his lips as his pants slid to the floor and his fingers trembled at the buttons of her skirt. When the last garments joined the others on the floor, they stood naked before each other, as though they were two innocent children, shy, tentative.

His gaze lowered to her mouth while his fingers slid gracefully over her waist, hips, bottom. It was as though he were a sculptor admiring his own finished masterpiece.

Carrie closed her eyes and exhaled a long, slow breath. Under the heat of his touch she felt a hot moisture traveling lower and lower. She wanted to reach out and touch him, but she knew her turn would come.

Strange. It didn't feel selfish just to stand there and take. His pleasure was transparent and the night was long.

Already she knew there would be a next time. Then it would be fast and urgent.

This would be their only first time.

And it would be perfect.

Fourteen

When Carrie finally reached out to touch Cash, his body no longer felt tense. His feet were parted slightly, and when she cupped his cold backside he seemed to meld to the palms of her hands. She rubbed him warm before she moved to his hips and onto his long, lean thighs. Shyly, she inched closer to the front, curious as to what she might find. When she finally gripped his rigid shaft, her gasp was lost beneath his groan. Wrapped around his girth, her fingers barely met, and when she stroked him she both marveled and worried over the size of him. But already the space between her legs throbbed, preparing the way.

He pulled her to him and she felt the wild pounding of his heart. Suddenly he lifted her off her feet, bringing her face even with his. She watched his lips coming closer and closer till they met hers... soft, wet, pliant. His tongue searched the recesses of her mouth and she clung to him, her need growing more urgent. Gasping for air, he lowered her down his moist chest, her legs parting on either side of his rigid sex. On tip toes she squeezed him between her thighs as he slid back and forth against her pulsing center. Her legs began to quiver, and she wondered how much longer she could wait to feel him inside her. She wanted this man. And she wanted him now.

Without warning, he set her away from him. She wanted to scream, "No, please. Don't stop," but she couldn't break the silence. It was as though they were living a fantasy, a fragile one that words would surely shatter.

But stopping wasn't what Cash had in mind. He lifted her in his arms and carried her to the bed, depositing her there gently. As he lowered himself to her, she watched the tenderness on his face and she knew, as she had all along, that she had been right to trust this man with all that she possessed.

Still holding her gaze, he slid between her legs, not penetrating, but rubbing along her feminine ridges, with long strokes that came quicker and quicker. His fingers worked her most sensitive spot, as the head of him dipped into her ever so slightly, teasing, testing, then pulling back. She wanted to reach down and shove him into her greedily, but closing her eyes, she waited, her heartbeat thundering in her ears.

His rubbing intensified and she trembled beneath him. Finally she tilted her head back and emitted a throaty sound she didn't recognize as her own. Streaks of silver and blue skittered behind her lids and her world spun out of control. Hot liquid trickled down her inner thighs. Unable to move, she heard the sounds of her own labored breathing and opened her eyes. When she thought she could take no more, he locked his arms on either side of her, his eyes fixed on hers, and rubbed every wondrous inch of himself over her silky wet entrance, still not entering her. On a groan, and with all the energy left in her, she sat up and cupped his face in both her hands. She claimed his mouth, her tongue tracing his lips with hot, wet strokes, before thrusting back inside for another taste of him. His firmness throbbed hot and hard against her belly, till suddenly he froze, holding her tight in his arms. Their chests pressed against one another's and they each gulped in air. Knowingly, she held very still, waiting for Cash to regain control.

When he had, he kissed her gently and laid her back down, spreading her legs wide with his knees. His velvety head had barely broken the plain when she felt her world tip sideways once again. He took her cue and penetrated a little farther, inching back, then forward, till finally she lifted her hips and he buried himself to her core. She held him tightly to her, exhausted but not wanting him to stop. His kiss grew deeper, hungrier. He groaned into her mouth as Carrie raised herself to him with each quickened stroke. At last she felt his muscles quiver and his hot seed spill into her. He breathed heavily into the side of her neck and she stroked his long, slick back, waiting for her own breathing to return to normal.

She lay there for the longest time trying to think, but all she could do was feel. He pulled her to him, molding the backs of her bent knees to the front of his, nestling his chin on top of her tangled hair.

When their body heat subsided, they crawled beneath the covers and curled into each other the same way, nuzzling closer, sinking farther into the pillows and cool, crisp sheets. Still, not a word had been spoken. There was so much to say, so much she wanted to tell him. But for now it would keep.

In those final relaxed seconds before she surrendered to sleep, Carrie thought she had never felt so complete. At last she had found the man she would spend her life with . . . someone she would love and cherish always.

Sunlight spilled through the window, tugging Carrie awake. At first she thought she must have dreamed their lovemaking, but then she swung her legs over the side of the bed and felt a swollen tenderness that reassured her it had truly happened. She yawned loudly and stretched, all the time looking out onto Union Square and the city below.

Wait a minute. What's wrong with this picture? She turned quickly and eyed the empty space behind her. Then she listened, hoping for the sound of the shower or other evidence that Cash was still there. Nothing. A lonely ache coursed through her as she realized she was alone.

The morning after. Were they about to have one of those? When she saw him next, would his eyes be full of regret? Or not even meet hers? She wanted to throw herself back on the bed and pull the covers over her head, but then she spotted the note on the dresser, propped against the base of the lamp.

Tentatively she walked over to it, afraid there'd be no words of love or tenderness, yet hoping she was wrong.

She wasn't.

If I don't run into you this morning—meet me at the valet station at noon.

What a romantic son of a bitch! She balled the note in her fist then slung it at the rumpled bed. Angry tears spilled down her cheeks as she raced for the shower.

Why? Why had she let this happen? And why had she let herself believe something special had happened last night?

Cash drummed on the steering wheel of his Mercedes and waited for Carrie. "What a fine mess you've gotten yourself into this time, Cunningham," he said aloud on a sigh. He checked his watch and looked up just as he spotted her walking toward him. Her stride was long and angry, her hair bouncing from side to side in her wake. The doorman ran to get ahead of her in time to open the car door. Without asking, he deposited her bag in the back. Quickly he stepped aside, accepted the folded bill she shoved in his hand, tipped his cap and shut the door behind her.

Carrie stared straight out the front window, arms folded tightly against her heaving chest. Cash accelerated slowly, merging onto Geary Street once they'd cleared the garage.

He drove through the city, forcing himself to concentrate on traffic and directions till they reached the freeway.

When he pulled onto 101 he straightened in his seat, preparing for the duel that was bound to come. He'd had all night and morning to think about what he'd say, but now, as then, nothing seemed appropriate. To tell her how special last night had been for him would only bring some scathing remark. If she only knew how difficult it had been to slip from beside her warm and trusting body, to lie in his own cold bed, staring at the ceiling till dawn. No matter what words he put to it, she was bound to feel used. Still, the bald truth was they couldn't do this again.

First, there was the policy against intercompany dating. He felt another twinge of guilt. Who had known the rule better than he when he entered her room last night, when he kissed her and held her in his arms, when he...

Cash set the cruise control and relaxed his legs, hoping the tension in his back and chest would ease as well, but it didn't. And he knew why. There was a bigger reason than that idiotic policy that had caused him to pull away from Carrie this morning. And it had to do with trust. For almost half of his life, he'd learned to trust no one but himself—at first for survival, but now the instincts were so deeply ingrained, he wondered if he could ever...

"Well?" Carrie said loudly, her posture unchanged.

Out of the corner of his eye, he saw her glance at him, then look away. He exhaled a loud sigh, wishing he had more time to think, but knowing he had to say something.

"Carrie... I'm sorry—"

"Oh, puhlease!" She crossed her legs and started swinging the top one.

"I know you're angry, and I don't blame you."

"Then why?" She turned sideways in her seat and, in the brief second he looked at her, he saw the sheen over her hurt green eyes. "What was last night all about?"

It had been about feelings he'd never felt before. Vulnerability, for one. And a oneness he never would have thought possible. It had been as though something, or someone, had brought them together. Pushed them, actually. He'd never felt so out of control, as if the whole experience had been orchestrated by a much more powerful hand.

This train of thought was foolish. He could have said good-night at the door, as he had the night before. But he hadn't. He'd wanted her. Needed her.

"I take full responsibility for what happened last night—"

"Great!" She turned back to the front and recrossed her arms.

He hated himself for the excuse he was about to give her—the only excuse he *could* give her right now, and one that might help just a little.

"Carrie, you know the rules. You wrote them. You—"

"*You*, Cash Cunningham. *You* wrote *that* rule. I simply copied it into the manual." She turned to him, and he caught her accusatory look. "And why exactly did you make that rule, Cash? Not every company has it. Has this happened before?"

He stepped on the accelerator, overriding the cruise control. He tried to remind himself this was his fault, but her tone was wearing on him.

"Well? Has it?"

"No. It hasn't." He could feel her stare, sizing him up for the truth. "Last night was—"

"Yeah, yeah. I know. *Special*."

He could almost taste the acid in the way she said the word. Yet as angry as she sounded, he knew this woman well. She was hurting. Badly. The fact that he was the one who'd inflicted so much pain twisted at his insides.

"I know you don't want to believe me . . . but yes, it was special." He stole a sideways peek and saw the tears ready to spill. Quickly she faced the opposite way and sniffed. "So special that if—" He couldn't believe he was saying this, but he knew it was true. "If we didn't work together, Carrie—" he swallowed his own pain and pushed on. "—I'd be on your doorstep day and night." He watched her back straighten. "But I don't see how we can break the rules that we ask everyone else to follow. Especially now, with the new policies . . . how delicate things are at the office . . . after the problem with Sam . . ."

Cash let his words trail off as he stared at the long stretch of highway in front of them. He wished they were home and he wasn't hearing her sniffle, knowing she was wiping her eyes, too. God, how he'd like to pull off the road and take her in his arms. Tell her everything would work out. But he couldn't touch her. Never again. He couldn't dare to feel what he felt. If he held her, he'd kiss her. Then he'd only want more. Not just the feel of her next to him, but the sound of her laugh, the smile in her eyes. Would he ever see that again?

"So we just go back to work—" she jammed a wadded tissue in her pocket "—and pretend nothing happened. Is that what you had in mind?"

"If I were simply an employee, I could leave my job and maybe—"

"Wait a minute! Are you suggesting I leave my job?"

She swung around in her seat, and for a moment he thought she might punch him. Both her fists were balled in her lap. Maybe if she did he'd feel better. "Carrie . . . you're the best thing to happen to the company in years. Please believe me. Your job is secure."

"Right. Bought and paid for." Her tone was hard and resigned as she slumped in her seat.

"Yes . . . by intelligence and hard work. Nothing more."

She didn't answer this time, but slid lower, resting her head on the back of the seat. When Cash glanced over, her eyes were closed. She didn't move or speak the rest of the way to Monterey, giving him plenty of time to feel like the total jerk that he was.

Since it was a Friday and nearly three o'clock when they arrived back at the office, Cash pulled alongside her Woodie and stopped. He didn't have to tell her she could go home if she wanted. There was no doubt she would.

He watched her open the door, retrieve her bag from the back and walk the few steps to her car, looking like a sleep-walker in a world of her own. Each movement was slow and deliberate, her expression blank, emotionless. No crinkles at the corners of smiling green eyes. No dimples. No spring to her walk, no bounce to her curls.

He watched another minute as she started her car and drove off, and wondered whether he would ever see Carrie Sargent again.

Fifteen

Carrie pulled an M. M. Day's T-shirt over her head, tucked it into her jeans and then went to work on her hair. A lot of mousse and a few growls later, she shook her head hard from side to side, letting her unruly curls fall as they pleased. With hands on hips, she appraised the red frizz in the mirror. If she couldn't control her hair, why did she think she could her life? She turned her back on her reflection. To hell with it. To hell with everything.

She stormed down the back steps and yanked the connecting door open and stopped short. Not far away, on a bar stool Fran was eyeing Gus over the rim of her coffee mug. Gus eyed her back with a cat-that-ate-the-canary smile. Carrie watched a moment, adjusted her attitude as best she could, then strolled over. Fran looked her way and patted an empty stool.

"Coffee or tea, m'love?" Gus asked.

"Oh, I think it's a coffee kind of morning," Carrie said, settling onto the stool beside Fran. Gus filled her mug, a

grin still fixed on his face. "Uh-huh!" Carrie began. "I go
out of town a few days, and look what happens!" She took
them both in with a smile that gave birth to a glimmer of
hope. Just because her love life was in shambles didn't mean
it couldn't work for someone else. She was so glad for them.

"Why, whatever do ya mean, lass?" Gus dried glasses
and kept his gaze on Fran. Fran blushed and blew on her
refill.

Whatever was going on, it wasn't her business. When one
of them was ready, she'd hear about it. In the meantime,
she'd borrow a little piece of their happiness and keep her
chin up.

"Lass...what are you doin' here on a Saturday...and all
dressed for work? Don't ya have some Christmas shoppin'
ta do?"

"Yeah, maybe later. Thought you might need a hand with
the lunch crowd...all those shoppers will be here any time
now." She looked at her watch: ten minutes till the doors
opened. A few patrons were clustered outside already.

"What's the matter? Lose your job?" Gus winked at
Fran, not having a clue how close to the mark he might be.

No, she hadn't lost her job. Yet. But how long could she
stay under the circumstances?

Carrie felt Fran's hand slide over hers. "Dear? Is something wrong? You and Mr. Cunningham didn't fight, did
you?"

No, worse. We made love.

Carrie picked up her mug and averted her eyes. "It was a
great workshop. In fact, we agreed on everything." *That had
to do with the company.* From the corner of her eye she
could see Fran and Gus exchanging frowns, but to their
credit, they didn't push for more.

Gus laid his towel on the bar, grabbed the keys and
headed for the front door. "Okay, lass. If we get busy, just
jump in anywhere. Keep Frannie company in the meantime."

"I love it when he calls you Frannie." Carrie poked her friend in the side.

"We've been seeing a lot of each other lately," Fran said, the color rising in her cheeks again.

"Really?" Carrie gave Fran's shoulder a squeeze and decided to stop teasing her and change the subject. "How are things at work? Any fallout from the Sam situation?"

Fran hesitated before she answered. "Sam hasn't shown up and we haven't heard from him. We can only hope he's seeking treatment. Everyone's been so worried about him. You can still feel the tension around there."

If you think there's tension now, just wait.

Carrie sipped her coffee and avoided looking Fran in the eye. How was she ever going to pull it off? People were bound to notice the change. If only she could talk to Fran about what happened. But she was Cash's loyal employee. She couldn't risk saying anything that might put her in the middle. Besides, Fran seemed happier than ever with Gus these days. Why spoil her holidays? It was bad enough her own were down the tube.

Carrie looked around the pub and noticed the decorations. "Excuse me a minute. Think I'll go plug in all the lights. Brighten this place up a little."

The booths filled first, then before long, all the tables and every bar stool. The waitresses who had once resented her now patted her on the back and thanked her for pitching in. It was nearly three o'clock before they got a breather.

"Thanks, lass. Ya've been a real help. Now why don't ya go buy me somethin' for Christmas?" He untied her apron, handed her the sweater she'd left behind the bar and gave her a nudge toward the door.

She sassed him as she moved along. "What makes you think I'm getting you anything?"

"Because ya'd be real embarrassed when I gave ya yours if ya didn't have somethin' for me." He turned and walked back to the bar.

Carrie laughed as she left the pub. But when she rounded the corner on Ocean Avenue she looked left and right, not knowing where to go first, and not really in the Christmas spirit. Crowds of holiday shoppers brushed by her and carolers could be heard from somewhere, probably the park. She headed toward the music, feeling more depressed than she had last night when she finally went to bed.

Men! When would she ever learn?

She dropped wearily on a bench on the corner of Ocean and Mission and listened to the music in the park behind her. How was she going to keep her job and face Cash day after day? The same questions that had haunted her in the middle of the night still went unanswered. Why had he let it go so far, if he didn't want it to continue? And why had she, when she knew how closed he was. Yes, she knew the rules.

She also knew the rules had nothing to do with Cash's actions Friday morning. It was as if the night had taken on a life of its own. At the time everything seemed so out of control.

Carrie pushed off the bench and headed for Carmel Plaza across the street. This wasn't like her—not taking responsibility for her own actions. She was a big girl. She'd known the risks. Now she'd just have to pay the price.

Monday morning, when she entered her office, Carrie closed the door behind her—something she'd never done before, but felt was necessary for a while. At least the first day. Maybe if she got through this one, the rest would be easier.

Dream on.

When Dwayne Flutie called at ten o'clock, he added to her despair. "Sorry, Carrie. I've looked everywhere, but I haven't been able to find anyone with Sam's qualifications. Can you hold on a little longer? Someone's bound to surface."

"Is there any choice?" Carrie asked on a sigh.

"Well…there was one possibility…." Flutie began, then paused.

"Yes?" Please! Something positive today.

"There's a gentleman in San Francisco with the experience, but he's looking for ownership, too. Either to buy someone out or possibly a partnership."

Right. Fat chance. "You'd better talk to Cash about that one. But I wouldn't hold my breath."

"Is he there?"

She'd heard him come in right after she arrived. She listened a second for signs of life on the other side of the adjacent wall. "Yes, he's in. Let me transfer you."

"Thanks, Carrie. If I don't talk to you before then, I'll see you Saturday at Cash's party. Have you ever been to his home? It's quite grand, you know."

Carrie stared straight ahead. The Christmas party. At Cash's. Great. She'd forgotten all about it.

"Carrie?"

"Oh…sorry, Dwayne. No, I've never been there." *She'd never even been to his house.* Tears welling, she quickly said, "I'll put you through to Cash now." She punched the right buttons, hung up the phone and swiveled to the glass wall behind her.

Oh, what a tangled web we weave…

What would the employees think if she didn't show for the party? The rumor mill had been alive and kicking the last time she noticed. Even if she was able to deceive the masses for the rest of the week, her absence Saturday would certainly warrant comment.

"Okay, S. Four and a half days plus one party. You can handle it." Next week would be a short week, since Christmas was on Friday. She'd grit her teeth and handle that, too. She pulled a form from her bottom drawer—a vacation request. She hadn't been here long enough to earn paid time off, but she could always ask for unpaid time. The worst he could say was no.

She scribbled out the dates and signed the form, all the time remembering the night they'd shared. She put down the pen, her thoughts lingering on their time together. He'd been so gentle, so loving. It had been everything she'd ever imagined and more.

She sprang from her chair and strode to the door. Enough. She'd ask for the week between Christmas and New Year's...without pay. Scrooge ought to like that. She'd spend that week thinking about her future, checking the want ads. If she worked up the nerve, maybe she'd ask for Dwayne's help. He wouldn't be pleased she was leaving Cunningham so soon, but better he earn another commission than someone else.

She stopped outside Cash's office and listened. He was still on the phone. She'd visit the little girls' room and muster up some more courage. After last week, looking him in the face wouldn't be easy.

Cash hung up the phone and tapped his mechanical pencil against a blueprint. If Flutie couldn't find a replacement for Sam, then it was doubtful anyone could.

He rocked back in his chair. But selling part ownership in the business to get a good man seemed a tad extreme. He wondered for a moment how much it would be worth. Nah. He straightened in his chair, prepared to concentrate on the prints in front of him, when he heard the knock on the door.

Damn. He'd been dreading this moment all weekend. There was no doubt who it was. It never occurred to anyone else to bypass Peg, especially when his door was closed. He puffed out his cheeks, then blew out loudly.

"Come in." He scribbled a note to himself, avoiding eye contact as long as possible. He could see her red skirt at the front of his desk. "Have a seat." He waited till she did, then glanced up. She was studying a paper in her hand, and his heart skipped a couple of major beats.

A letter of resignation? He felt miserable. Just as he had all weekend. When she slid the paper in front of him, he realized what it was and started breathing again.

"I know it would be without pay," she began, "but I'd like that week off." Her voice was an octave lower than usual, with none of the typical emotion he'd come to expect.

Cash scribbled his name on the authorization line and handed it back. Still no eye contact. Somebody had to make the first move. If it had to be him, so be it. "Look, Carrie . . . we're both adults here, and—"

She stood unexpectedly. "The past is the past. I don't see any point in rehashing it." Unlike earlier, her voice was loud and strong.

At long last he braved a look. She was staring out the window beyond him, her mouth set in a grim, straight line. She looked as uncomfortable as he felt and something more. There was a sadness around her eyes.

When the silence became unbearable, he said, "I need you to get a memo out to the supervisors today . . . about the EAP."

"Okay." She didn't move or look his way.

"Tell them there's a meeting at four tomorrow. Someone from Performance Consultants is coming in to show them a video and explain how to spot problems, deal with employees, make referrals. . . . Well, I don't have to explain it to you."

"Is that all?" she said to the window.

"Just one more thing. Peg says you haven't RSVPed for the party Saturday. Are you planning on going?" He could lie to himself, but he knew what answer he wanted to hear.

"Why? Am I uninvited?" Finally she turned and faced him, her icy daggers hitting their mark.

So . . . some of the spunk was still there. Somehow that made him feel better. "Of course not. Peg just wants the final count before she calls the caterers back."

"Okay, I'm going." She paused for a moment. "Can I go now?"

Since when did she ask his permission to do anything? Was this how it would be from now on? Short and curt? Not a word to spare? For some reason he wished he could think of a reason to detain her. There were so many things to be said, yet there wasn't a word that would fix what had happened.

"Yes…you can go now." He watched her turn and leave, shutting the door behind her.

This was never going to work.

But how…and when…could he let her go? Not from the job, but from his life? When was the last time he'd felt anything remotely close to what he experienced with this wily woman? He tossed his pencil down, and it rolled across the blueprint and fell on the floor. And to add to the mix it was nearly Christmas. He'd heard his employees call him Scrooge behind his back, but he wasn't as thick-skinned as they thought. He thought of Sam and just as quickly blocked it out. Then there was the party Saturday.

God, the party. He raked his fingers through his hair, wishing he could pound his fist through the wall instead. The last thing he felt like throwing right now was a party.

Sixteen

"**T**hanks for letting me tag along with you two," Carrie said from the back seat of Gus's Explorer.

"No problem, Carrie girl. We're glad to have you."

Fran looked over her shoulder from the passenger seat and smiled before returning her adoring attention to the driver.

Carrie tried holding on to their happiness, but the closer they got to Cash's house the worse she felt. If contractions were anything like the pains in her stomach now, she wasn't sure children would be part of her future.

Nonsense, she told herself. She knew that wasn't true. Why was she making such a big deal out of this? The house would be crowded. There would be plenty of people to talk to, spouses to meet. So she'd see Cash from time to time. That didn't mean she had to linger with him.

Or think of the wondrous things he'd done to her mind and body just a week ago.

Right!

Gus pulled into the long drive and Carrie let out a gasp. "Is this it?" She looked behind her, and from the crest of the hill she could see the Pacific Ocean, thinly veiled by pines and cypress branches. A light fog hung over a cluster of boulders, and whitecaps were visible in the distance.

Gus parked and Fran eased out of her seat. "This is it." She opened Carrie's door. "Isn't it something?"

Carrie stepped out and stared at the sprawling Victorian in front of her, replete with flounces and furbelows in perfect condition. The home had to be over a hundred years old, but by the look of its freshness it could have been completed yesterday. Dark olive trim gave way to taupe in places, framing the warm, creamy off-white exterior. Bay windows, turrets—a veritable feast for the eyes.

With a slack jaw, Carrie breathed in the crisp ocean air and followed Gus and Fran up a stone walk bordered by the bold red-and-green V-shaped leaves of ice plant. A rock garden here and there broke the long, landscaped slope leading to an inviting oval leaded-glass door. She stopped at the wraparound porch steps and looked up at the turret to the north, with its circular stained glass near the top. Angled on the southwest corner was a dormer above a large first-floor window, its glass tucked behind crisscrossed diamond shapes.

"Are ya comin', lass?" Gus stood at the entrance, holding the door. Fran had gone inside.

Carrie closed her mouth and climbed the steps. This was nothing like the cold, contemporary offices of Cunningham Construction. She'd half expected lots of glass and brass, with paintings that would make her wonder if they were hanging upside down or sideways. As she passed through the oak-floored vestibule and a uniformed woman took her coat, Carrie's gaze traveled to an antique umbrella and hat stand, then passed to a highly polished bannister winding its way to the second floor. Handel's *Messiah* played in the background, sending a shiver down her arms and back.

They weren't the first to arrive, she noticed, and was immediately grateful. A large decorated pine tree filled a bay window at the far side of the parlor to her right. Slowly she worked her way through the crowd, pasting on a fragile smile and nodding to those she knew as she crossed to the tree.

"Many are nineteenth-century German." The voice came over her shoulder, and she turned to find Dwayne. "Some English and a few French, I believe." He cradled an ornament in his hand and studied it. "This one's German," he pronounced with a decisive nod of his head.

Carrie tore her gaze from the tree and eyed Flutie. "I'm impressed," she said.

Flutie straightened his tie and feigned modesty. "Oh, well, I'm something of an antique buff myself."

"No, I mean...well, that Cash would care enough to own such things." She swept her arm out to include the entire room. "This house—" She shook her head, speechless.

"If you recall, I warned you it was exquisite." Dwayne rocked on the heels of his shoes a couple of times, seeming proud of her surprise and acting as if it were his own. "Carrie," he began hesitantly, "I got the message late yesterday that you wanted to talk with me." Deep furrows appeared at the bridge of his round, wire-rimmed glasses.

Carrie scanned the area for anyone in earshot. Satisfied that they couldn't be heard, she said, "Yes. I'd like to make an appointment with you...as soon as possible." She watched his lips pucker and knew his worry was justified. Then she saw Cash crossing the room and her heart began racing. He wore a creamy fisherman's knit sweater over khaki pleated pants—a page out of *GQ*, looking every bit the lord of the manor and totally relaxed.

This wasn't right. Something was wrong with this picture. The man she'd fallen in love with was back—warm, genuine, giving. He moved from cluster to cluster, shaking hands, smiling, saying a few words. She'd almost convinced herself that the man in San Francisco had been a myth, a figment of her overactive, romantic imagination. But here he was again. In all his splendor.

And she wanted to cry. She wasn't on his arm. Soon she wouldn't be in his life.

"Carrie?" Dwayne moved in front of her, blocking her view. "Is there something you wanted to tell me?"

She closed her eyes for a moment, exhaled, then looked at Dwayne's troubled face. "Yes." She patted his hand and forced a smile. "But not here. It can wait. Let's talk next week, okay?"

Dwayne held her gaze long enough to know what was coming, and he didn't hide his disappointment. "Yes. Of course," he said, and moved on.

A man from the shop took the opportunity to approach her, a pretty brunette clinging shyly to his arm. "Carrie...I'd like you to meet my wife, Jeannie," he said, smiling lovingly at the woman affixed to his side.

Carrie took the petite fingers in hers and returned the timid woman's handshake. "It's nice to meet you, Jeannie."

"Jeannie and I wanted to thank you personally for what you've done for us." The foreman shifted his weight from one foot to the other and stared at the floor. "I mean...well, you know...the EAP."

Jeannie stood taller and finished. "We lost our first baby last summer." She bit her top lip a second, then rushed on. "It's been a difficult time...so we made an appointment with an EAP counselor." Jeannie smiled bravely. "She's real nice. We went together yesterday, and I'm going to go alone next week. I already know she's going to help me." Jeannie looked around, seeming self-conscious once again. "Anyway...thank you. We just wanted you to know it's a good thing you started."

Carrie swallowed and tried to find her voice, but all she managed was a slight nod before they walked away.

She had to find the bathroom before she made a fool of herself. She walked toward the back of the house and found one unoccupied. Quickly she stepped inside, shut the door and leaned against it. Tears trailed down her cheeks, and she closed her eyes to stem the flow. She was sad for Jeannie's loss, but that wasn't all. It was this place. The holidays, the music.

And Cash.

What was she going to do about Cash? She couldn't work with him day in and day out without going crazy. Regardless of what he felt—or, more appropriately, didn't feel—she was in love with the man. No ifs, ands or buts about it. She was a goner.

She walked over to the oval mirror that hung above a white pedestal basin and looked herself in the eye. Pathetic. Not just her red eyes, but her aching heart. How had she let this happen? "You've really gone and done it this time, S." She took a tissue from her pocket and dabbed carefully at her face and under her lashes, careful not to smudge her mascara. Then she blew her nose and squared her shoulders. Somehow she'd get through this day.

Her hand hesitated on the doorknob as she let out a long breath. She'd avoid Cash as much as possible, mingling with employees, finding Gus and Fran if need be. When she thought she'd spent sufficient time here, she'd find Cash, thank him and leave.

Only one problem. She didn't have Woodie with her. Well, okay. She'd call a cab if Gus and Fran wanted to stay. There. That was a good plan. Now she was ready. She turned the knob and opened the door. A few yards away she saw Cash, and she shut the door again.

So much for the plan. She counted to fifty and tried again. Through the narrow opening she spotted Fran and Gus this time. He was kissing her forehead and gazing down at her tenderly. They made loving look so easy. She waited a while longer, till Gus left. Slowly Carrie opened the door the rest of the way and walked toward Fran, who turned and smiled.

"Don't you just love this house, Carrie?" Fran's gaze swept the dining room behind her.

"Yes. It's very beautiful." She hadn't meant for her voice to betray her. When Fran turned to her again, Carrie averted her gaze. "The caterers are doing quite the job. Everything is so organized, and the presentation is a work of art." She could feel Fran's curious stare, but she ignored it and crossed to the crystal punch bowl. Before she could help herself, a uniformed waiter extended a silver tray with filled cups. She took one along with a holiday napkin, thankful for something to occupy her hands. She sipped slowly and scanned the area. More guests had arrived, and the one person she dreaded seeing was nowhere in sight.

Eventually she found herself in a cluster of friendly faces. She laughed and nodded in all the right places and felt the tension start to ebb. The merriment had risen to such a level that she couldn't hear herself think—which she thought was a lifesaver under the circumstances. Restless, she decided to do a little exploring.

Carrie eased herself from the crowd and wandered to the back of the house. She passed an open door and peered in. It was a warm yet distinctly masculine library. Built-in shelves rose to the ceiling and were covered with hardcover books. On a leather-padded bench under a bay window, a couple held hands and stared out at a cluster of pines and eucalyptus. She tiptoed passed the door and found a large country kitchen with glass-paneled cupboards and hand-painted knobs. In the center of the room was a large work-station with a cutting-board top. Caterers, hard at work re-placing empty platters, seemed not to notice her arrival.

She crossed to the cozy breakfast nook beyond them and slid into a ladder-back chair facing another rock garden and propped her elbows on the table. Resting her chin on her locked fingers, she gazed out at the peaceful sight, relishing the reprieve. She noticed a side door that opened onto a small porch. Before she could look farther, she saw two large poinsettias bobbing in the crosspaned window of the

door. A dark brown jacket hung from a tall body barely
visible behind them, the face obscured by the flowering
plants. She looked around wondering who else might get the
door, but saw no one who wasn't carrying a tray. There was
a light knock on the door, sounding more like a shoe kicking the bottom. The plants bobbed some more and Carrie
stared at them. Who would be making a delivery after the
party started? If it was a guest bringing presents why didn't
he come in the front like everyone else? The kick came again
and she pushed out of her chair, irritated with the intruder
and not at all comfortable playing hostess for Cash's party.

She opened the door and a muffled "Thank you" came
from behind the plants. He moved to the table and deposited the pots, then turned around.

"Sam! What are you doing here?" She looked over her
shoulder. The kitchen was empty. Slowly she inched backward, her eyes never leaving Sam. He took a step toward
her, and she jumped back farther.

He held up both hands, a weary look in his eyes. "Carrie...please don't run off. I'm so sorry for everything, for
the way I treated you."

He kept his hands up and she noticed they were not
shaking. She looked more closely at his eyes. They weren't
bloodshot, as they usually were, but simply sad and tired
looking. Still, why was he here? She knew he hadn't been
invited. To be on the safe side, she walked backward into the
kitchen.

Sam motioned behind him to the poinsettias as he followed her. "The white one's for Cash. I know they're his
favorite. The red one's for you," he finished while staring
at his boots. "Thought you seemed more the red type."

He moved closer and Carrie inhaled discreetly. No obvious signs of liquor. He acted calm, nothing like the last time
she'd seen him. If fact, the sneer she usually saw was gone,
too.

"Sam!" Cash came to an abrupt halt in the doorway, his
square jaw tight, his eyes livid. "What in the hell do you

think you're doing here?'' Before Sam could answer, Cash moved to Carrie's side. ''Are you okay?''

The warm, caring man from San Francisco was back in a flash. His hand rested on her arm protectively, the warmth of his touch penetrating her red angora sweater. She looked up at him, feeling his breath on her face. ''Y-yes. I'm fine.'' *Except that you're touching me and looking at me as though you care.*

''Cash—'' Sam said, breaking her trance, ''—don't worry. I won't cause a scene. Honest.''

''What do you want, Sam?'' Cash said, not moving from Carrie's side.

''I want my job back.''

''You've got to be kidding!''

''Please,'' Sam said, holding his hands up again. ''Just hear me out.''

Cash moved back to the door leading to the dining room and shut it, then started pacing in front of it, looking angrier than Carrie had ever seen him.

''I haven't had a single drink since…since—'' Sam looked from Cash to Carrie, then back to Cash, letting the sentence go unfinished.

Cash stopped pacing and stood toe-to-toe with Sam. ''You've got family, man.'' He gripped the older man's shoulders and shook them hard. ''You've got *kids*,'' he shouted in Sam's face. Then, dropping his hands, Cash moved backward till he bumped into the chopping block.

Carrie watched Cash's chest heaving beneath his sweater. He gripped the counter behind him and lowered his head. She could see him fighting for control. More than anything, she wanted to go to him, to tell him she understood. She knew exactly where his thoughts were. And she knew it hurt. Badly.

Beyond the closed door others began singing, adding a surreal backdrop to the painful drama unfolding in front of her.

Siiilent night . . .

"You of all people, Sam," Cash said in a barely controlled whisper. "You're one of the few who knew how it was for me as a kid—a teenager worried about where I'd live, how I'd make ends meet all by myself." Cash's head snapped up. Pain mixed with anger radiated from every inch of him as he glowered at Sam. "You know *exactly* what killed my parents and left me fending for myself. And it wasn't a boating accident, was it?"

Hoooly night...

"No, Cash, it wasn't." Sam stared straight ahead, unable or unwilling to make eye contact.

"Then what was it, Sam? Tell me."

All is calm...

Sam turned away, his shoulders beginning to shake. "It was the booze," he said in a raspy voice. "It was the booze."

All is bright...

Cash folded his arms and closed his eyes. The voices rose in the next room, the music wrapping a silent haze around the threesome. Carrie listened to the words of the song and prayed they would bring a measure of peace to this tense little room.

Finally Sam turned and faced Cash. "There've been problems at home I haven't told you about—"

It was Cash's turn to hold up his hands. "Stop right there, Sam. As much as I'd like to, I can't fix those problems. I'm not a counselor. My job is, and always has been, to focus on your performance."

Carrie felt the tension seeping from her limbs. It was going to be okay. Cash had read PC's manual. The words were almost verbatim...

"As to your performance, Sam..." Cash shook his head, and Carrie saw the sadness in his eyes. "There's no room for substance abuse at my company."

Sam looked at his boots again. His arms hung limp at his sides. "You're right, Cash. I screwed up. Big-time." He raised his eyes but not his head. "I'll do whatever I have to... if you give me another chance."

Carrie watched the conflict behind Cash's eyes and knew what he was thinking. Sam was a good man, a talented craftsman. But could he be trusted to follow through? From what she had just seen and heard, Carrie thought he could. Silently she watched the pair sizing each other up, neither looking away from the other.

Sleep in heavenly peace...

When Cash let his gaze travel to Carrie, she knew what he was asking, just as she always had whenever he let himself be honest with her. She held her breath and returned his gaze with a tender look, one she hoped he would understand.

"Sam..." Cash heaved a sigh. "Would you agree to see an EAP counselor?"

Sleep in heavenly peace...

Sam straightened to his full six-foot-plus height. "Yes, sir. First thing Monday, if they'll let me."

"You'd have to be screened for drugs and alcohol on a regular basis to prove to me you're sticking with the program."

"Of course, of course," Sam said. Taking an optimistic step forward, he extended his arm to Cash. "You have my word on it, Cash. I won't let you down...again."

Cash looked at the hand a moment, then stepped closer and gripped it firmly, holding the older man's steady gaze.

Sam pumped Cash's hand unceasingly. "You won't be sorry, Cash. Thank you." He looked at the ceiling. "Oh, God, thank you." He backed out of the room, half tripping over his own feet, before scurrying out the back door.

Carrie let out the breath she'd been holding. Cash had made the right decision; she was sure of it. Sam would go to the EAP, and maybe the rest of his family would, too. Whatever their problems, Christmas was bound to be brighter for Sam and his family, thanks to... She'd almost used the word *Scrooge,* but she hadn't. She never would again. When she looked up, she met Cash's tired eyes and her heart did that uneven-rhythm thing again, just as it always had when he showed her this side of him.

"Do you think I made the right decision?" he asked, cautiously closing the distance between them.

"About Sam?" she asked, knowing very well that was what he meant. "Yes. I think you did." She could see in his eyes that he hadn't missed her reference to other matters.

Why had she said that? It was hopeless, pointless.

"Your home is beautiful, Cash," she said, playing with a chipped nail and avoiding those puppy-dog eyes trained on her.

"Thank you." His hand trailed gently down the sleeve of her sweater, stopping when he clasped her fingers. "But none of this will mean a thing come Christmas morning—" he squeezed her hand "—with no wife or children to share it with."

Gus pushed through the door. "There ya are. We've been lookin' all over for ya two. Mind steppin' into the livin' room for a minute? Got a little surprise."

Cash held firm to Carrie's hand, but didn't move. "Give us a second, Gus. We'll be right there."

Gus gave a thumbs-up sign and left them alone.

"Carrie." Cash looked down at her with such intimacy, such intensity, that she could do nothing but stare back at him. "There has to be a way to work this out. I've been so miserable— "

"Me, too. But—"

"I've had an idea, but I need some time. Can you give me a while?"

She heard herself say, "Yes," without explanation. It didn't matter *how*. Just *what*. For the first time since San Francisco, she dared to hope.

"Come on." He tugged at her elbow and smiled at her lovingly. "We can't keep Gus waiting. Let's go see what this surprise is all about."

Seventeen

Carrie squirmed under the comforter, finding just the right dips in the mattress, then exhaled a long sigh.

"What a day," she said aloud, shaking her head, still feeling as though she'd just come out of some epic dream. First the thing with Sam, then Gus and Fran's engagement announcement! What wonderful news that was!

Then there was Cash.

She let her thoughts drift for a while, remembering his face in the kitchen—first when he thought she might be in danger, then when he'd asked her to give him time.

She sat up in bed and pulled the comforter under her chin. Time for what? No matter how many times she asked herself that question, she always came back to those damnable company rules. She threw the covers off and began pacing her small apartment.

If only she'd taken Woodie to the party this afternoon, then maybe she and Cash could have talked things out when everyone left.

Right. She laughed at her own fabrication. Talking would have been the last thing on the agenda. And lovemaking wouldn't have changed the facts.

She stopped at the narrow window and gazed down at Ocean Avenue, seeing nothing but Cash's face. Had she stayed, would she be in his bed right now? She rubbed her arms and turned from the window.

What was Cash up to? The only aboveboard way they could be together, without causing upheaval at the office, was for her to leave her job.

She stood very still, a sudden awareness streaking through her, chilling her to the bone.

Leave her job . . . leave her job.

The words reverberated in her head, sending excitement dancing along her nerve endings. That had been the answer all along, hadn't it? When she thought Cash was suggesting it on the drive home from the conference, she'd been furious.

And blind. And stupid.

She went to the refrigerator, pulled out a can of diet Coke and popped the top. After a long pause and a few swigs, she resumed her pacing.

Waiting had never been her strong suit. She had to *do* something about this situation. Now! Besides, why put them both through the time and torture when she held the key? After all, what was more important to her? Her job or a life with Cash Cunningham?

The choice was simple. She loved this man. No doubt about it! And after today's events, she knew the feeling was reciprocal.

She stopped pacing and drank more Coke, recalling her decision to look for a new job between the holidays. At the time that decision was made, she'd felt sad and beaten. Now she felt exhilarated. She loved her job . . . but not nearly as much as she loved the boss.

Carrie flopped down on the edge of the sofa bed and smiled. She could get a job anywhere, but she'd never find a man like Cash, not if she spent the rest of her life looking. She finished her Coke, set the can on the floor, and slid back under the covers.

The plan started unfolding in her head, slowly at first then gathering speed. Her heart pounded in her chest as she passed each hurdle. She locked her hands behind her head and recounted the details, arranging an order to her list of things to do, a chuckle erupting from deep in her throat.

After church tomorrow, she would go see the travel agent. If she remembered correctly, he opened at noon on Sundays. She had met him a few times downstairs at the pub—a real friendly sort, always sat at the bar, often trying to talk Gus into getting away, taking advantage of some special or other.

She just needed one little ticket. Standby, if necessary. Her flight would have to leave late tomorrow afternoon and get her back before work on Monday. It might cost her a pretty penny with such short notice. She smiled. It would be worth it.

After the travel agency she would go to the office and hope Cash wasn't there. He'd given her the combination to his safe some time ago, since there were documents they shared that he preferred be secure. If she knew Cash, the papers she needed would be there, too.

Yes, they would be. She could feel it in her bones.

All she had to do was get in and out of his office without getting caught. Getting things out tomorrow might be easy. Putting them back Monday might present a challenge. But, hey, it was all part of the adventure. She loved surprising people, and this one would be a lulu.

She rolled onto her side and felt her concentration start to ebb. Her last waking thoughts were of a long white limousine and the look on Cash's face when he stepped inside.

Carrie bounded down the back steps early Sunday morning and ran directly to Gus, who was behind the bar restocking shelves. She threw her arms around his shoulders and squeezed him hard.

"Ooo... I'm so happy for you and Fran," she said, rocking him from side to side. "Have you picked a date yet? Am I invited?"

Gus laughed over her shoulder before stepping back to eye her, his head cocked to one side. "My, my... aren't we chipper this mornin'? Ya've been moonin' around here all week. Now look at ya!" He set a bottle of Jack Daniels in its place. "I like this look much better, lass."

She noticed he didn't answer her questions. Instead, he seemed more interested in the source of her newfound happiness. She would have loved to have shared her plan with him, but not yet. For now she would keep her own counsel. Gus maintained his curious stare.

She checked her watch. Service at the Mission started in twenty minutes. She didn't want to be late. A perfect start for a perfect day, she told herself. "Gus...in case I don't get to talk with you later, I want you to know I probably won't be home tonight... so don't worry."

His bushy eyebrows shot up, a devilish know-it-all twinkle in his eyes. "Is that right? Well... have a good time, lass... whatever it is you're not tellin' me."

"Look who's talking? I don't recall you answering *my* questions, Gus McGee." She winked and started for the door. "God sure works in mysterious ways, doesn't He?" Carrie called out as she reached the entrance.

"That He does, lass. That He does."

Monday morning Carrie dragged herself out of Woodie and rubbed her aching back. As hard as she'd tried, she hadn't gotten a wink of sleep on the plane. Adrenaline had pumped through her all day and night as she worked through the first steps of her plan. Everything had gone like clockwork.

She filled her lungs with cool salty air and trudged from the parking lot to her office, her limbs numb with exhaustion. The excitement was still there, but it was currently buried under sleep deprivation. She hung her coat on the back of the door and then dropped into her chair. From the other side of the adjacent wall, she could hear Cash's muted voice. She smiled and rocked back. If only he knew what she was up to. . . .

The phone rang and she picked it up. "Good morning. Carrie Sargent."

"Good morning, Carrie Sargent."

Damn. Dwayne Flutie. She should have known he would call first thing. Yes, she needed help finding a new job. But she didn't want Cash to know she was looking. Not yet.

"Dwayne . . . I'm sorry. This is a very hectic week for me. Would you mind if I got back to you after Christmas?"

There was a slight pause, and she thought she'd heard a sigh of relief.

"Actually, that would be perfect. Merry Christmas, Carrie." He hung up without another word.

Now what was that all about? She stared into the receiver before replacing it in its cradle. She'd thought he would be worried sick about her leaving Cunningham before his commission kicked in, that he'd try to talk her into staying. Something. Anything. Merry Christmas and goodbye? That was strange even for Dwayne.

Oh, well. She shrugged and opened her briefcase, extracting the documents she'd borrowed from Cash's safe. Sometime today she would put them back. Maybe lunchtime. She would find out from Peggy his schedule for the day and be sure she had sufficient time. She'd come this far; she didn't want him ruining her surprise now.

Cash's office door was still shut when she passed. A tingle ran down her spine just thinking of the man on the other side of the door. More than anything, she wished she could burst in, drop on his lap, and plant a big, sloppy kiss on his sexy lips. She smiled and kept moving, gathering the information she needed from Peggy before working her way to the coffeepot, and then Fran's desk.

Fran rose to greet her, a wide smile lighting her petite features. Carrie pulled her into a tight embrace, then stood back and saw the glow in the older woman's face. "It's wonderful, Fran. I've never seen Gus happier." Fran sat down and dabbed at her eyes while Carrie picked up her mug and drank some much-needed caffeine. "So when's the big day?" If Gus wouldn't tell her, maybe Fran would.

Fran looked on either side of Carrie, then leaned closer and whispered, "I'm not supposed to tell anyone, but Gus forgot that I have to give you a vacation request form." She opened her center drawer and produced the paper.

Carrie read the dates and swallowed a chuckle: between Christmas and New Year's. Cunningham Construction might as well shut down that week, with all the requests that had crossed her desk, her own included.

"Do you think there'll be a problem with such short notice?" Fran asked, looking worried.

Carrie waved the form at her and smiled. "Not to worry. It's bound to be a slow week, anyway. I'll talk with Cash today. I'm sure he'll approve it."

Fran held a hand over her mouth, looking as though she were hiding an uncontrollable laugh. The mischief in her eyes gave her away.

"Come on . . . tell me, Fran. I can keep a secret."

Fran looked around again, then motioned for Carrie to come closer. "We're eloping!" She hunched her narrow shoulders. "Lake Tahoe . . . New Year's Eve. Isn't that romantic?"

Carrie bent and kissed Fran on the cheek, then gave her another hug. "I'm so happy for you both." She started to leave, then remembered something. "Oh, Fran . . . do you happen to have a portable sewing machine I could borrow?"

"Why, yes, I do. I'm going home for lunch to play with Fefe. Would you like me to bring it in this afternoon?"

"That would be great. And one more thing . . ." This was going to seem strange, but she crossed her fingers behind her back and braved the request. "Do you have a navy blue blazer or suit jacket I could borrow till after New Year's?"

Fran said, "Sure," without as much as a question. She was still giggling like a schoolgirl when Carrie left her cubicle and sauntered to the coffeepot for a refill.

Back at her desk, Carrie shuffled through paperwork, doing what was absolutely necessary and stalling for time till Cash left for his luncheon appointment. Peggy had said he would be gone for at least two hours. She'd said Cash himself had penciled in the appointment this morning before she arrived. She also said he was acting sort of weird, to beware.

Just before noon Carrie heard Cash's door open. She listened and waited, wondering what he would do when he passed her office. She hadn't seen him since the party, which, now that she thought of it, seemed odd. After the way he looked at her Saturday, and his encouraging words, she would have thought he would seek her out this morning, if for no other reason than to say hello. His footsteps retreated in the opposite direction and then she heard the ding of the elevator. He rarely took the elevator. Was he trying to avoid her?

Nah. Something was going on, but it wasn't bad. It couldn't be...not after what *she'd* started in motion. She wouldn't allow such negative thoughts. As eager as she was to talk with him, to feel his arms around her, she knew the further along she was in her plan, the better.

She got out of her chair and walked cautiously past Cash's office, peering around the corner at Peggy's desk and the elevator. Peggy was gone, too. The phone rang twice and then stopped. The answering service was on.

Perfect. She would return the items to Cash's safe and no one would be the wiser.

By the time Cash left the restaurant, the sun had burned off the fog, and brilliant rays sparkled on the surface of the water as he drove south to the office. He took this as a good sign. Carrie and sunshine were back in his life. And soon something else would be: the small business he'd always wanted from day one.

The papers hadn't been penned yet, and there would probably be a little dickering over the final price, but in his mind it was a done deal. Flutie said the guy was good for the financing and eager to make a move. He'd made a favorable first impression, too. Not too pushy, good questions and a definite knowledge of the business. The employees would like him.

Funny. When Flutie had first told him someone might be interested in buying all or part of Cunningham Construction, he'd rejected the idea. But that had been before the party. A few moments with Carrie in the kitchen and it suddenly seemed crystal clear what had to be done. On the surface it seemed extreme to sell the company, but in reality it was what he'd wanted all along. He would be free to restore his old ladies, Carrie could keep her job, and they could be together.

Still, he knew it was more than that. At long last he had learned to trust someone other than himself. And, finally, he could stop running and smell the roses. When his parents died and he'd discovered they had mortgaged everything for their sick life-style, that there was nothing left to see him through, he'd scrambled for years to support and educate himself, to keep his head above water. Except for the money he'd put into restoring his own home, he'd squirreled away every spare penny for so many years that he'd never stopped to notice it was no longer necessary.

A smile curled his lips as he parked his car and strode inside. He couldn't wait to see the look on Carrie's face when she learned what he'd done. He'd have loved to tell her now, but he didn't want to jinx the deal. He'd wait till he had a formal purchase offer in hand, then he'd tell her. With his attorney's and Flutie's help, maybe they could get it done by the end of the week. What a perfect Christmas gift...for both himself and Carrie.

He ran up the back stairs, worrying about two little details. How would he find out her ring size, and could he get one sized by this Thursday, Christmas Eve? He snapped his fingers as he raced down the hall.

Gus. He could help find out the size . . . even if it meant sneaking into her apartment when she wasn't there and finding her jewelry box. With the odd assortment of earrings and doodads he'd seen her wear, she had to have a jewelry box. He passed Carrie's empty office and chuckled aloud. Nothing was going to stop him now. Not even a little breaking and entering.

He was about to enter his office when he saw Carrie strolling down the hall toward him. He met her halfway and smiled, longing to pull her in his arms. Carrie came alongside him with an impish look on her face, and they went into his office. She dropped into a chair across from his desk as he walked behind it and sat down.

He rocked back in his chair, still smiling. How was he supposed to get anything done this next week with this gorgeous creature close by? He sat up and started shuffling papers on his desk, finding it easier to concentrate with his eyes down and his hands busy. "I've been meaning to tell you about all these notices from suppliers who'll be shut down between the holidays—"

"Oh, here," she said, interrupting, handing over the form dangling from her fingers. "Almost forgot. This one's from Fran." Cash took it and added it to the pile in front of him. She looked molded to the chair, ready to nod off any minute. After the party, he'd expected something else from her today. For a second, he questioned whether he'd read her wrong last Saturday, then he gave a mental shrug. No. There had to be another explanation for her lethargy. Maybe she'd spent the weekend Christmas shopping or helping Gus.

When he didn't respond, she added, "I hope there aren't too many."

Cash pulled himself back to the conversation. "No, not at all. Actually, I've decided to shut down... give everyone a long holiday." This got a small rise out of her, but not much. There was a faint smile on those luscious, full lips.

"I'll get a memo out to all departments right away. Thank you, Cash. That's very sweet of you. I know everyone will be thrilled."

He cocked his head and studied her. How could she sit there and act as if this were any other day? As if she were any employee?

"I'd better get busy," Carrie said, pushing off the arms of the chair. "With only three work days left, we'll all be pushed to the max to get everything done by Thursday afternoon."

If only she knew how true her words... But as she started to leave, he worried again if her feelings for him were as strong as he'd thought.

"Oh! Another thing I almost forgot to tell you—don't make any plans for Christmas Eve or Christmas Day." She walked out the door, calling over her shoulder, "You're spending that time with me."

Cash let out a relieved sigh and smiled at the empty doorway.

She thinks she's so clever. Wait till she hears what I've got up my sleeve come Christmas Eve.

"We'd better hurry. If Carrie catches us in her room we'll both be mud. Ya know that, don't ya?" Gus fumbled with the spare key in the lock and let Cash pass in front of him.

All they had to do was find one little ring, trace the opening and be gone. Gus flicked on an overhead light and Cash stopped short. A sewing machine was perched on the small dinette table. A shopping bag labeled "Carmel Fabrics" lay next to it.

"Well, what do you know? She sews." Another surprise he could add to the list. Carrie was full of them. He shook his head and laughed. Maybe that's where she got all those outrageous outfits she wore to work.

"Here it is," Gus whispered, handing a jewelry box to Cash. "You open it. I don't feel right 'bout it." Then he looked up at Cash and winked. "But I do like the reason for this little caper. Guess I'd better... since I'll be in the same boat sooner or later."

The older man looked as happy as Cash felt. He'd been right earlier, when he'd thought next year would be better than ever. Fran and Gus. Himself and Carrie. A new business. How quickly things had changed.

"Will ya get a move on? Ya making me nervous."

Cash found a ring and traced it on a blank page in his pocket planner. Quickly he replaced it in the box and left the small apartment, feeling more than a little smug.

Carrie deposited her load of packages on the floor of her apartment and heaved a sigh. The sewing machine loomed larger than life in front of her. She groaned aloud. "Not tonight."

Tomorrow would be soon enough. Right now she needed a long hot shower and a good night's sleep. She flung her jacket over a dinette chair and headed for the bathroom. At least her Christmas shopping was done. There was still wrapping to do, but she didn't want to think about it now. She couldn't have thought about another thing if her life depended on it. The energy it would take to strip and shower and crawl beneath the sheets seemed work enough.

She turned on the shower head and waited for the water to warm, amazed that she did have another thought—the same last thought she'd had Saturday night when she'd started putting her plan together.

The long white stretch limousine.

She giggled and stepped under the hot spray. The driver would arrive Thursday afternoon, Christmas Eve, at four o'clock. She'd already typed her letter of resignation that she planned to give Cash once the vehicle was on the road. She turned her face into the spray and smiled. The letter was the least of what she planned to give him...in the back seat of that limo.

Eighteen

Carrie arrived early Thursday morning, feeling as though she'd already had her fifth cup of coffee. She darted past Cash's door, thankful he was nowhere in sight. Once inside her office she closed her door and leaned against it, struggling to catch her breath. As soon as she had, she hid her battered brown suitcase under her desk and dropped into her chair. Quickly she ran through its contents in her head. *The navy blazer and new navy skirt, her letter of resignation in one envelope, the rest of the papers in a second envelope, all her toiletry articles, even a disposable razor and new toothbrush for Cash, as well as his Christmas gift...*

Yep. It was all in order. Even her special props. She started to giggle, wishing she could start her plan now, instead of at four o'clock this afternoon. She hoped the day would be busy, that the time would fly. Yet how could it? She'd already organized her files and made notes for her replacement, whoever that might be. How would she spend the next eight hours?

Carrie sprang out of her chair, coffee mug in hand, and headed for the break room. She spotted Fran the second she turned the corner. The woman appeared as frazzled as Carrie felt. Maybe a little chitchat was what they both needed to calm their nerves.

"Got all your presents wrapped, Fran?" Carrie waited for her turn at the coffeepot.

"Oh, my, yes. Over a month ago." She looked around to be certain they were alone. "Good thing, too. I'd be worthless at it now—what with everything that's going on."

"Having second thoughts?" Carrie asked, filling her mug and slanting Fran a grin.

"About Gus? Not at all. Just nervous…excited, I guess. It's been a long time since…" She started to blush and didn't finish her sentence.

Carrie wrapped her free arm around the small woman's back and squeezed her shoulder. "It's great Cash gave us next week off, isn't it? You'll have plenty of time to pack and plan your trip."

Fran let out a short laugh. "I'm afraid that's done, too. Even found a neighbor to keep Fefe. All I have to do now is wait. It's the waiting that grinds on you, you know."

Ah, yes. She knew well.

"Of all the years for Mr. Cunningham to give us the week off. I would have preferred to keep busy." She frowned as they left the room together. "Wonder what prompted him to do it? We've always worked that week."

"Maybe he's mellowing with age," Carrie said with a chuckle.

"I don't know." Fran stopped and slowly rotated the mug in her hands. "He's been acting awfully strange this week— the few hours he's been here." She looked up at Carrie. "Have you noticed the change?"

In truth, she'd been so preoccupied with her own agenda she hadn't paid close attention. "Actually, I haven't had much contact with him since the party." What *had* he been up to all week? Whatever. After today it wouldn't matter.

Carrie stooped to give Fran a hug. "In case I don't see you later, you and Gus have a super Christmas."

Fran returned Carrie's hug and spoke over her shoulder. "I wish you were spending the day with us, but Gus told me you have other plans." She pulled back slowly. After the slightest pause, she planted a gentle kiss on Carrie's cheek. "Merry Christmas, Carrie. You've made this year so special for me." A ridge of moisture hung precariously at the rims of the older woman's eyes.

"Now don't you go crying on me, or you'll have me starting." Carrie swallowed the lump in her throat and laughed as Fran gave her a chest-high wave and turned away.

Carrie walked back to her office feeling a little sad. As excited as she was at the idea of being with Cash later, she would miss seeing Fran every day, and the other employees, as well. She'd liked this job more than any other she'd had. Even the one at her father's business. There she'd been the boss's daughter. Here she was simply herself, judged and accepted on her own merit.

She passed Cash's open door and stole a peek. He still wasn't in. And by the looks of his desk, he hadn't been in earlier, either. She retraced her steps to Peggy's desk. "Peggy...do you know when Mr. Cunningham will be in?"

"He called a little while ago. Said he was at his lawyer's office and expected to be there most of the day." She leaned closer to Carrie and whispered, "He sounded pretty harried."

"Did he happen to mention he had to be back by four o'clock?"

Peggy shook her head. "Sorry. Can I help you with something?"

Carrie exhaled loudly. Surely he'd be here by four. She'd made a point of telling him she'd made plans and that they'd be leaving then. "If you hear from him again, will you put him through to me, please?"

"Will do."

The phone rang and Carrie seized the opportunity to escape to her office. She was worrying over nothing, she kept telling herself. He'd be there.

He'd better be.

At 3:30 she started pacing the floor of her office. Cash still hadn't arrived and he hadn't called back.

At ten to four Peg's voice came over the intercom. "Do you know anything about the limousine out front?"

Carrie raced back to her desk and pressed the button on her phone. "Yes, I do. If the driver comes in, tell him to wait. Any word from Mr. Cunningham?"

"Not a word."

"Let me know the second you see him."

"Okeydokey."

Carrie pulled the suitcase out from under her desk. It was time to change clothes. "Cash Cunningham . . . if you don't get here soon—after all I've gone through for this moment—you're dead meat."

She closed her door and locked it, then began to strip, all the time listening for sounds of life on the other side of the wall. Where was he, anyway? What was so important that it took all day? On Christmas Eve, no less.

She finished and stored her work clothes in the suitcase, then checked her watch for the umpteenth time: 4:10. Now she was getting angry. She went to the door and yanked it open, falling back a step when she did.

"Cash! Where have you been?" Harried was right. His hair was windblown; he looked short of breath. But then he let out a long sigh and smiled at her in a way that said all was well with the world.

"I'm sorry I'm late. I'll explain everything later, okay?" He took her by the shoulders and gazed down at her tenderly, evaporating the head of steam she'd gathered.

"Okay," she said, eyeing him curiously. Then she remembered the driver downstairs. "Did you come in the back or the front?"

"The back. Why?" He cocked his head and raised an eyebrow. "What are you up to, Carrie Sargent?"

"I told you. I made plans...starting ten minutes ago. Remember?"

Cash looked at his watch. "I was going to make the rounds and wish everyone Merry Christmas...but I suppose most have already left." Apparently seeing the look of distress on her face, he smiled and said, "Just give me two minutes, then I'll meet you at the front door." His gaze suddenly drifted down the length of her. "A navy suit? I didn't think you owned such a thing!"

Carrie smirked and placed her hands on her hips. "Will you hurry up, please?"

He saluted her and did an about-face. "Two minutes."

Carrie looked at the office behind her and sighed. She'd made it a cozy place, and she loved her view of the ocean from their perch atop Monterey. She walked to her desk, picked up the suitcase behind it and said goodbye to it all as she left her office for the last time.

After a short stop at the ladies' room, she strolled through the lobby, stopping in front of the massive pine tree, remembering the smiles of her fellow workers as they found homes for their ornaments and sang along with the Christmas music, looking fresh and perky in their new logo T-shirts....

"Ready?" Cash appeared beside her, his arm circling her waist as if that were an everyday occurrence. She looked over her shoulder and caught the smile on Peggy's lips before she picked up another call.

"Is that for us?" Cash asked, nodding toward the limousine.

"Oh, I don't know," she teased, taking his hand in hers. "Why don't we go find out?"

The driver stepped from the long white vehicle and held open the back door. Carrie quickened her step, holding her hand out to greet him.

"You must be Derrick," she said, shaking his hand.

"Good afternoon, Miss Sargent," he said with a wide smile.

"Carrie," she corrected. "Please call me Carrie." She turned to Cash, who didn't seem the least bit surprised she'd ordered a limo. "And this is Cash."

Cash extended his hand, and Derrick's jaw dropped. "You're putting me on, right?" He looked from one to the other. "Cash and Carrie?"

"No, you got it right, Derrick." She winked and slipped him a folded note with a recap of her directions. She was leaving nothing to chance, least of all their privacy in the back seat.

Derrick chuckled. "Want me to put your suitcase in the trunk?" He reached for it, and Carrie clutched it to her chest.

"No. This stays with me."

He backed up. "Okay, Miss...Carrie. Let me know if there's anything else you need. Otherwise you won't be hearing from me till—"

Carrie held an index finger to her lips and Derrick stopped talking. He tipped his cap, smiled, and shut the door behind them. When they started moving, Carrie saw the dividing window close behind him. She pulled the short velvet curtains shut for added measure. Then she settled back in the soft leather seat and sighed. Cash took her hand in his and she stared at his long, graceful fingers. She couldn't believe the moment was finally here.

"This is a very nice surprise, Carrie. After the day I've had, this is just what the doctor ordered. It doesn't even matter where we're going." He smiled wearily down at her, pulling her closer to his side.

"Good. Because I'm not telling you." She kissed his cheek, feeling as though she'd burst with happiness.

"Another surprise?"

"Oh, yeah," she said, and started to laugh. "More than one."

He looked at her suitcase, then back to her face. "Will we be stopping at my place for a bag?"

"Nope. I have all we need right in there." She pointed to the old brown bag and laughed again. Snuggling against his shoulder, she said, "You were going to tell me where you've been all day."

He squeezed her to him. "All in good time, my love."

My love. Two simple words that sent a chill careening through her.

"I will tell you that I went over to Sam's."

"Really! How's he doing?"

"He's seems happier than I can remember in years . . . thanks to you."

"You mean thanks to the EAP," she said, feeling embarrassed at all the credit.

"Who talked me into the EAP?" He smiled down at her and she felt certain she'd dissolve in his arms any moment. "In addition to counseling, PC directed Sam to a local Alcoholics Anonymous group, and his family's going to Al-Anon, too. I think he's going to make it. He's eager to get back to work."

"I'm glad. I know how much the company needs him, how much you've missed him."

"I think this will be a very special Christmas for Sam . . . not to mention Fran and Gus. You must have had a hand in that, too."

"Maybe a tad." She chuckled. Then she nodded toward the bottle of champagne chilling in a bucket. "How 'bout a toast to the happy couple? Shall we start with a little bubbly?" She reached for the bottle, but he pulled her back, circling his arms around her.

"I'd rather start here," he said, pressing his warm lips against hers.

Carrie leaned into him, returning his hungry kiss with a passion she'd never felt before. His tongue searched intimate corners of her mouth, and she felt her blood rushing, hot and thick, to needier parts. She kept telling herself to take it slowly, savor the moment. They had hours ahead of them. Yet her body screamed for more. Hard. Fast. Now. The weeks since their time in San Francisco had been filled with torturous nights and frustrating days. At every turn she had tried to act as though she didn't care—a nearly impossible feat. Now the restraints were gone.

With the last of her willpower, she broke their kiss and pulled back. She saw his stunned expression. Maybe this was the time for dialogue, but the language of his eyes transcended words. He'd left little doubt at the party, and now, as to how he felt.

She'd never been what she considered the aggressor in lovemaking, but this night would be like no other. It was time for action, time to let him see what she'd only dreamed of all week.

Before he could pull her back, Carrie knelt on the floor in front of him and removed his shoes. She freed his belt and zipper with lightning speed, her eyes never leaving his as she tugged his pants and briefs to the floor, slinging them playfully aside.

Cash spread his arms out on the back of the seat and eyed her steadily, waiting for whatever came next. But when she ripped off her breakaway navy skirt, revealing red garters and strategically placed mistletoe, he threw his head back and roared.

When he regained his composure, he asked, "You sewed that skirt yourself, didn't you?"

"Yes," she said proudly, then wondered why he sounded so certain.

"Carrie, Carrie," he said, between bursts of laughter. "What am I going to do with you?"

Hunching over in the short space, she placed one knee on either side of his thighs, laughing along with him. She loved to see him laugh from his belly. His eyes were bright and happy, the lines on his forehead gone. He was still laughing when she cupped his face and kissed his smiling lips. But not for long. Their chuckles turned to groans as she kissed him deeper, harder, their heavy breathing quickly fogging the interior of the dark tinted windows.

"Just love me, Cash," she said breathlessly a moment later. "Just love me."

He stroked her cheek and smiled with his eyes. "That I do," he whispered, his warm breath falling on her cheek. "I think I've always loved you . . . probably from the first moment you ran into—"

She pulled back and slapped at his chest. "Who ran into—?"

"Okay, okay. Since the moment we ran into each other. Is that a fair compromise?"

Instead of answering, she went to work on the buttons of his shirt, kissing each inch of revealed flesh as he gently eased the blazer from her shoulders. When nearly all their garments had joined the pile on the floor, Cash pulled her to him, kissing the hollow at the nape of her neck, moving his moist lips lower, over the swell of her breast. Beneath her she felt his firmness pressing against the damp space between her legs. She kissed the back of his lowered head, wondering how much longer she could wait till she felt his fullness inside her.

His lips returned to hers and she met them greedily, pushing him sideways till their bodies stretched along the seat. Wearing nothing but her red garter belt and dark hose, she straddled his thighs and caressed his rigid shaft with long, light, increasingly rapid strokes. When she could wait no longer, she impaled herself, sinking inch by glorious inch down on him. Finally he thrust upward, burying himself to the hilt, caressing her backside with those wondrous fingers of his.

Carrie felt the tears trailing down her cheeks as hot liquid poured out of her and onto his belly. Cash pulled her to him, his chest rising and falling in rhythm with hers, his deep thrusts coming quicker and quicker. Their mouths melted together, completing the union, lust and love colliding full force. She could feel her tears wetting his cheeks as specks of shooting light rocketed behind her closed lids. Just when she thought it was over, Cash slowed his pace and eased her onto the floor, rolling her onto her back.

Suddenly the glow of the small dome light behind his head surrounded him and a little voice deep within her said, "This is the man you waited for, Carrie." It was exactly how she felt, what she knew was true. But the words and voice seemed like someone else's—a familiar but long-forgotten one.

"I love you, Carrie . . . and I always will."

It took a couple of heartbeats to realize that the voice she now heard belonged to Cash. He lowered himself to her and kissed her lightly.

"I love you, too, Cash . . . with all my heart." Consecrated love flowed from his beautiful blue eyes. Out of all the world, she knew she had found the right one. She wrapped her arms around his back and took him deeply into her soul and her body, feeling him shudder against her a moment later.

Nineteen

When Cash rolled onto his side, he took her with him, not breaking their oneness, stroking her back, uttering sweet sounds of contentment.

Carrie shivered, feeling a sudden chill dance over her bare skin. She sat up and drew the cumbersome suitcase closer, raising the lid ever so slightly. Withdrawing her grandmother's handmade afghan, she relatched the case quickly and pulled the crocheted yarn over their moist bodies. Satisfied, she snuggled back into Cash's embrace.

"Is there anything you didn't think of?" he asked, kissing her forehead and shifting his weight to his back.

"I hope not," she said.

"What else do you have in there?"

She sat up abruptly, taking the cover with her. "Oh! I forgot. There's something I can show you right now." She looked over her shoulder at him. "In fact, I think it's a perfect time for you to read this." She opened the case a slit and extracted the thinner of the two envelopes. Then she lay down again, tucked the cover over both of them and handed him her letter.

Cash unfolded the single sheet of paper and read it silently.

He sat up with a start, this time taking the cover with him. "What?" He turned and faced her, angry lines pinching the bridge of his nose. "You're not quitting. No way." He refolded the paper and tore it three times before tossing it aside. "You have to stay. You're the glue that will hold it together."

Carrie sat up and crossed her arms over her breasts, anger and hurt warring in her chest. "So what was this all about? Another one-night stand?" In spite of her efforts not to cry, tears spilled down her face. She swiped at them, glowering at the set of his jaw. "You can't make me stay. I'm not going to sneak around to be with you...and I'm not going to spend another day in that place wishing I could touch you and knowing I can't."

Cash started to pull her to him but she stiff-armed him.

"Stop being so hot-tempered and listen to me a minute," he said.

What was the point? Then again, where could she hide? She lifted her chin a notch and turned sideways. Cash reached for his suit coat at the bottom of the pile in the corner and pulled a document from the breast pocket. "Will you at least read this before you throw me out of a moving vehicle?"

She snatched the paper from his hand and caught sight of his cocky grin. How could he be grinning at a time like this? Didn't he know how she felt about him, how much more she wanted from him? Slowly she focused on the words in front of her. She read it twice, not believing her eyes.

"Cash! You can't sell the company. It's your life."

He took the purchase offer and slipped it back in his coat. "No, it's not." He kept the coat next to him but turned to Carrie. "You are."

"But—"

"No buts. Assuming the purchaser's financing is approved—which Flutie assures me will be the case—it's a done deal. That's why I was a little late."

She stared at him incredulously. "What will you do?"

"Return to my old ladies—restore Victorians. With this sale, I can afford to do whatever I want . . . including marrying you."

She continued to stare at him, not believing her ears. Her job *and* the man she loved? On a long sigh, she closed her eyes and offered a silent prayer of thanks. She'd read him right after all. He was ready for the commitment he'd hinted at the day of the party. She opened her eyes slowly and looked at the man she'd spend the rest of her life loving. How could she have doubted, for even a second, how much he cared?

When she saw the smile tugging at the corners of his lips, she crossed her arms and looked down her nose at him. "Haven't you forgotten something?"

"No," he said confidently, lifting her backside onto the seat. He let the afghan fall to the floor and knelt naked in front of her, pulling his jacket to his side. Without his gaze leaving hers, he reached into the jacket pocket, hiked up one knee, then clasped Carrie's fingers around a black velvet box.

"Carrie Sargent . . . will you do me the great honor of being my bride?"

"Of course," she said, forcing the words past the lump at the back of her throat.

Cash opened the box and slipped the two-carat diamond on her third finger. She held it up to the light, its brilliance matching the wonder she felt at this miraculous moment. Nothing in her elaborate plan could rival Cash's proposal. She pulled the ring closer and studied it, then slanted a look at his smiling face.

"How did you know the size?"

He shrugged. "Just lucky, I guess."

She knew none of this had anything to do with luck. It was divine intervention. "It's perfect, Cash. Just like you."

He laughed and reached for the bottle of champagne. "*Now* I think it's time for a toast." He uncorked the bottle and poured two fluted glasses, handing one to Carrie.

"To my little drill sergeant. I know it's spelled differently, but that's what you are just the same."

"The spelling of my last name is of little importance," she said, lifting her chin as she clinked her glass to his. "Since it won't be Sargent for long."

"Exactly how long are you going to make me wait?" He asked, taking a sip from his glass and eyeing her. "I suppose you'll want the big white dress and the whole nine yards. How long will it take to arrange all that? We could have the reception at my... our house."

"Yes, we could. That's a wonderful idea. I love your house."

"Our house," he corrected.

"That won't be hard to get used to!" She laughed. "But as far as the rest, don't you think you're rushing things a bit? I've barely said yes to your proposal. What's the hurry?"

"I can't believe I'm saying this...but I can't wait. I don't want to spend another night in that big house without you." He hugged her hard, then pulled back and looked her in the eye. "We could always live together while we're working out the details—"

"Stop right there, cowboy. I'm no prude, but I am old-fashioned. You're just going to have to wait till we're married before a single one of my things crosses that gorgeous threshold of yours."

"Did anyone ever tell you you're stubborn and inflexible sometimes?"

She punched playfully at his shoulder, sending him backward on the seat, his glass tumbling to the floor. "Inflexible, huh? Well—" she bent over him and kissed him hard "—wait till you see this, then tell me again how inflexible I am."

Carrie awoke with a start when Derrick's voice came over the rear speaker near her head.

"Fifteen minutes till estimated time of arrival," he said, a chuckle at the end of his words.

Carrie pushed the button and answered, "Thanks, Derrick. Don't forget to tell me when you're pulling in, okay?"

"Yes, ma'am," he said with another chuckle.

Cash groaned alongside her and came awake slowly. "Where are we? What time is it?"

"It's time for another surprise." She rolled over and gave him a quick kiss, then opened the suitcase and pulled out a large flat wrapped package. "I meant to give this to you earlier, but you distracted me."

Cash accepted the present with reticence. "Carrie...I didn't know we'd be gone overnight. Your Christmas gift is at home under the tree."

She kissed him on the nose and nudged the package closer. "Don't be silly. What could you possibly give me that could top tonight?" She held up her ring and studied it again, marveling at Cash's impeccable taste and timing. "Come on. Open your gift. We don't have much time."

"You mean there's more after this?"

She smiled and flicked an impatient finger at the package.

Cash tore into the wrapping, unveiling a large pictorial book of Victorian homes—a gift she'd had no idea would seem so appropriate. She still couldn't believe he would be leaving Cunningham Construction, but she knew by the look on his face that he'd made a good decision, and that she'd found the right gift.

He pulled her to him, hugging her long and hard. "You're incredible. Thank you, Carrie." He sat back and eyed her tenderly, making her forget for a moment the task at hand.

Derrick's voice came over the speaker again. "We're pulling in, Carrie. Only one car in front of us."

"Thanks, Derrick."

"Let me guess. We're at a fast-food drive-through." Cash smirked. "Great. I'm starved."

Carrie laughed and opened the suitcase lid all the way. "Close, but no cigar. I'm afraid we won't have time to dress," she said, laying everything out around them. "Just sit up on the seat and we'll cover up with the afghan."

Cash looked at the items on the floor, then stared open-mouthed at Carrie.

"Well?" she said, prodding him. "Unless you want Derrick to roll down the side window and show the world your many attributes, I'd suggest you get a move on."

Dumbstruck, Cash did exactly as he was told. Carrie snapped a red-and-green plaid bow tie around his neck, then settled the short green veil on her head, the crown of which was adorned with twigs of holly. Quickly she hiked the afghan up, tucked it securely under their arms and handed Cash the last remaining manila envelope.

"When the guy asks, just give him this. Everything's there."

"Ready?" Derrick said as they started to roll forward.

"Let's see." She looked around frantically, taking inventory aloud. "Something old—afghan. Something new—my ring. Oh, dear. Something borrowed, something blue." She retrieved Fran's navy blazer from the heap and put it around her shoulders. "Think I can count this twice?"

"Why not?" Cash laughed and shook his head.

Carrie pressed the speaker button. "Ready as we'll ever be, Derrick," she said, fighting down a giggle.

The dark tinted window slid down slowly. Before they could see the person behind the glass wall, his deep vibrato voice warbled a loud refrain of "Love Me Tender."

The arched sign over the Elvis impersonator preacher read Nevada's First Hunka Hunka Love Drive-Thru Wedding

Chapel. Cash laughed through the rest of the song while Carrie struggled to keep the afghan in place.

When the song ended, the black waterfall hair bobbed a couple times as the preacher asked for the necessary documents. Cash handed over the envelope, still shaking his head in disbelief. The vows were mercifully short, but nonetheless sweet. Marriage certificate in hand, Carrie told Derrick to drive on.

They were still laughing and kissing a mile down the road, when Cash finally leaned back against the seat and sighed.

"Life will never again be dull. Of that much I'm certain." He pulled her onto his lap and wrapped the afghan around them. He lifted his wrist to the light and read the time. "Merry Christmas, Carrie Cunningham."

She snuggled closer. "Mmm... I like the sound of that name."

"You know, you were awfully sure of yourself to plan such a stunt. What if I didn't go along with it?"

She fell silent for a moment, enjoying the warmth of his body against hers. What if he hadn't? She'd never planned for that contingency. "Did you ever have a feeling that someone else's hand was at work on us?"

The dome light overhead blinked twice, then held steady. They watched it for the longest time, waiting for it to happen again, but it didn't.

Finally Cash answered her question. "Only from the moment you ran into... we ran into each other."

Carrie turned her head up to him and smiled. "Merry Christmas, you lucky devil." Cash threw his head back and laughed. It was a sound she'd never grow weary of hearing.

Carrie closed her eyes and silently sent another greeting.

Thank you, Mama. I love you, too.

*   *   *   *   *

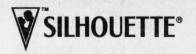

WHO'S THE BOSS? Barbara Boswell

Man of the Month

When masterful Cade Austin inherited 49% of a company and Kylie Brennan was heir to the other 51%, Cade planned to buy her out and send her on her way. Instead, he found he was battling it out—in the boardroom *and* the bedroom!

RESOLVED TO (RE)MARRY Carole Buck

Holiday Honeymoons

When thieves broke in to Lucy Falco's office on New Year's Eve, she was stunned when she was tied up with her ex-husband, Chris Banks! It wasn't long before they discovered how steamy their passion still was...

THE YOU-CAN'T-MAKE-ME BRIDE Leanne Banks

How To Catch a Princess

Remembering his wickedly handsome grin, Jenna Jean knew that former bad boy Stan Michaels was *not* husband material. Stan thought otherwise, but there was only one woman the confirmed bachelor considered *was* wife material—Jenna Jean!

GEORGIA MEETS HER GROOM Elizabeth Bevarly

The Family McCormick

Georgia Lavender had thought Jack McCormick would always be around to protect her from her father—then Jack disappeared. Now, finally, he'd returned to rescue her—and found she'd turned into a beautiful, sophisticated woman. Now *he* was the one in danger!

PRACTICE HUSBAND Judith McWilliams

Joe Barrington was not a marrying man. But when Joe found himself teaching his friend Addy Edson how to attract a husband, would Addy's practice kisses lure him to the altar?

THE BABY BLIZZARD Caroline Cross

Loner Jack Sheridan enjoyed his solitary life until a snowstorm stranded him with expectant mother Tess Danielson. Now he was forced to look after Tess and her new baby until the snow—or his heart—thawed.

FOUR FREE
specially selected
Desire™ novels
<u>PLUS</u> a Mystery Gift
when you return this page...

Return this coupon and we'll send you 4 Silhouette® romances from the Desire series and a mystery gift absolutely FREE! We'll even pay the postage and packing for you.

We're making you this offer to introduce you to the benefits of the Reader Service™– FREE home delivery of brand-new Silhouette novels, at least a month before they are available in the shops, FREE gifts and a monthly Newsletter packed with information, competitions, author pages and lots more...

Accepting these FREE books and gift places you under no obligation to buy, you may cancel at any time, even after receiving just your free shipment. Simply complete the coupon below and send it to:

THE READER SERVICE, FREEPOST, CROYDON, SURREY, CR9 3WZ.

EIRE READERS PLEASE SEND COUPON TO: P.O. BOX 4546, DUBLIN 24.

NO STAMP NEEDED

Yes, please send me 4 free Silhouette Desire novels and a mystery gift. I understand that unless you hear from me, I will receive 6 superb new titles every month for just £2.40* each, postage and packing free. I am under no obligation to purchase any books and I may cancel or suspend my subscription at any time, but the free books and gift will be mine to keep in any case. (I am over 18 years of age)

D7YE

Ms/Mrs/Miss/Mr ....INITIALS.................................

BLOCK CAPITALS PLEASE

SURNAME..

ADDRESS..

....

....POSTCODE................................

COMING NEXT MONTH FROM

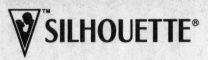 **SILHOUETTE**®

Sensation

*A thrilling mix of passion, adventure
and drama*

MUMMY BY SURPRISE Paula Detmer Riggs
THE BADDEST VIRGIN IN TEXAS Maggie Shayne
TEARS OF THE SHAMAN Rebecca Daniels
HAPPY NEW YEAR—BABY! Marie Ferrarella

Intrigue

Danger, deception and desire

HOTSHOT P.I. B. J. Daniels
WED TO A STRANGER Jule McBride
THUNDER MOUNTAIN Rachel Lee
LULLABY DECEPTION Susan Kearney

Special Edition

Satisfying romances packed with emotion

HUSBAND BY THE HOUR Susan Mallery
COWBOY'S LADY Victoria Pade
REMEMBER ME? Jennifer Mikels
MARRIAGE MATERIAL Ruth Wind
RINGS, ROSES...AND ROMANCE Barbara Benedict
A DOCTOR IN THE HOUSE Ellen Tanner Marsh

Barbara

DELINSKY

THE DREAM

She'd do anything to save her family home.

Jessica Crosslyn was prepared for the challenge of saving her family's home—but she wasn't prepared to share the project with Carter Malloy, a man she loathed. They could work together to restore the house, but mending past mistakes proved to be more difficult.

"When you care to read the very best, the name of Barbara Delinsky should come immediately to mind."—Rave Reviews

1-55166-061-X
AVAILABLE FROM DECEMBER 1997

GET TO KNOW
THE BEST OF ENEMIES

the latest blockbuster from TAYLOR SMITH

Who would you trust with your life? Think again.

*Linked to a terrorist bombing, a young student goes
missing. One woman believes in the girl's innocence
and is determined to find her before she is silenced.
Leya Nash has to decide—quickly—who to trust.
The wrong choice could be fatal.*

—

Valid only in the UK & Ireland against purchases made in retail outlets
and not in conjunction with any Reader Service or other offer.